Bathed in Blood
Dark Desires & Sinful Sweethearts Book One
Callie Moss

Copyright © 2024 by Callie Moss

All rights reserved.

No part of this publication may be reproduced, distributed, or transmitted in any form or by any means, including photocopying, recording, or other electronic or mechanical methods, without the prior written permission of the publisher, except as permitted by U.S. copyright law. For permission requests, contact authorcalliemoss@yahoo.com

The story, all names, characters, and incidents portrayed in this production are fictitious. No identification with actual persons (living or deceased), places, buildings, and products is intended or should be inferred.

Book Cover by Pretty in Ink Creations

Editor Alexa at The Fiction Fix

Contents

Dedication		V
Epigraph		VI
1.	Breeze	1
2.	Hunting	16
3.	Punishment	23
4.	Stream	30
5.	Taken	37
6.	Placement	45
7.	Gilded	49
8.	Flux	58
9.	Allies	68
10.	Bedmates	77
11.	Fist	86
12.	Heart	92
13.	Backing	97
14.	Implosion	102
15.	Scream	109
16.	Nothing	115

17.	Fall	123
18.	Jacket	126
19.	New	135
20.	Vanegas	142
21.	Family	147
22.	Found	153
23.	Spring	163
24.	Summer	169
Afterword		172
Bathed in Blood Playlist		173
Also by		174

Dedicated to all the disturbed romance lovers out there. May we never get our shit together enough to stop reading this garbage. Seriously, I'll be out of a job.

Trust is a strange thing. It starts as a dent in well-formed armor. The armor you build around yourself to protect all your spongy insides. It's a little dent in an otherwise flawless façade. What damage can a little dent do after all? The answer is a lot. That little dent marks the way for the axe before it's driven into your heart.

   -Lana

1
Breeze

<u>Limbo by Freddie Dredd</u>

Mom always told me that the ferocious way I loved the people was admirable, that someone who loved with their entire being was rare. She said I'd make an amazing wife and mother someday. To me, love never felt like a steady burning flame. No, it felt like an unyielding explosion. As I grew, I realized just how wrong she was, how loving like this was painful more times than not. I loved suddenly, deeply, and I *ached* deeply. Mom admired it anyway, so I never tried to change it, never made so much as a move to protect myself from... myself, from what that undying, selfless kind of love does to a person.

I always knew my little brother was her favorite. Lewis needed her doting in a way I never did, so I understood, even when it took away from what time she and I had. Truth is, I adored him too.

Almost as much as her.

With his shaggy, caramel colored hair, the way he refused to let it be brushed, but insisted upon keeping it long; what was there not to love about the way he unapologetically followed every whim he had the moment it popped into his head? The way his golden bronze eyes looked at everything like a door waiting to be opened, consequences be dammed.

He was her baby boy, her fierce ray of sun. Me? She said I was like the breeze on days her sun was shining too brightly. I made the fierceness of the sun bearable. I was the best big sister ever; he told me so himself. It was a role I took seriously.

Maybe that's why it was so easy that day to sign my life over for his. It wasn't even a question in my mind; I didn't take even a second to consider the consequences.

When I rushed into that godforsaken parking garage and saw Lewis on his knees, bloodied and terrified, all I could see was the bright eyed, headstrong toddler who needed his big sister to kiss his skinned knee and then swear to never tell his friends. He was the little boy who ran through the woods behind our house and climbed the biggest tree he could find. I didn't see the man he had become, those golden eyes swallowed by his pupils, his young face aged by years of hard addiction. I didn't see the track marks that lined his arms or the way his hands shook.

He was my little brother.

I should've left him there that day, my love soured by the times he'd stolen from me, hurt me and Mom in a drug induced rage. I should've remembered the night the very men who held him hostage broke into our home looking for him. How their hired muscle beat on Mom. How terrified I was, how my throat burned from screaming. I didn't think of any of those things. All I felt was that stupid, unyielding, explosive love. I thought of how hard Mom would cry. It would kill her as surely as they would kill him once they wrung him dry. She was nothing without that little boy, but me?

I was the breeze.

I tug the straps of my negligee up high onto my shoulders, the expensive black fabric hugging the generous swell of my hips, the deep neckline ending just below the line of my breasts. The sudden, sharp sound of a fist beating on a thick wooden door didn't startle me.

Little startles me these days.

"Come in."

The heavy door opens with the same ominous creek you hear in horror movies, the ones where the damsel's chest is heaving under the weight of her fear as she cowers inside the closet, her hand clasped tightly over her mouth in hopes it would stifle her sobs. The killer's heavy footsteps taunt her from outside the veiled safety of that closet. It's not a matter of *if* he finds her, but *when*. She knows it, the audience knows it, but we sit on the edge of our seats, anyway.

"We're set." Vince's voice is as cool and collected as ever, a strange contrast to his volatile, hell spawn brothers.

I fluff my deep red curls, making sure they fall perfectly over my shoulders as I pull my mask into place. This isn't a movie. There's no damsel, only killers. And me? I think I'm the worst of them all. The first time I made this walk is an ever-present weight on my chest. I can still feel the way my heart pounded in my chest as tears streamed down my cheeks. Anton called it my christening, and Jax lounged against the stone wall of the basement, the axe resting over his broad shoulder like a threat. He laughed, said it was *"time to break in the cunt"*. He's never called me anything but *just* that.

The cunt.

He told me the watchers would love the pitiful tears that leaked out from underneath the mask they forced into my trembling hands.

He was right.

They loved me.

I remember the way I sobbed as I made the first swing. I remember how much more terrifying the axe was after I saw the way a human skull exploded under the weight of it. My first swings weren't strong enough; I was timid, and my victim paid the price as I found my footing. The sound the woman made as the axe lodged itself into her head is a permanent fixture in my mind. I didn't know it then, just how much worse things could get. I had no clue it was the day of my rebirth. The day I became *her.*

The Blood Princess.

Bits of the woman splattered my mask while bits of my vomit splattered the inside. I was royalty. A myth. A legend. The next few years dragged on like entire lifetimes. I was more than a sister held to pay off a debt, more than just their prisoner now. I was a fucking cash cow, bringing in one point two million dollars per stream. I lost count of how many lives I took after that first year. At some point, I'd stopped crying. The nights were filled with such tormenting monotony, I'd even started looking forward to coming up with new, more graphic ways to rile up the viewers. I learned what the human body could take.

What it couldn't.

It was somewhere in the third year when I realized they would never let me go, that the carnage would never stop as long as I remained *her.* The bullet I'd assured myself would come any day now for two entire years was a pipe dream. I lulled myself to sleep every night thinking of the ways they would kill me on stream, dreaming of the night my karma would finally come calling. The Blood Princess' Final Show sounded like a good name. Theatrical—Jax would like that.

I'd deluded myself into thinking that was rock bottom. It was short-lived, and soon after that first year, I plummeted all over again. My soulless walking corpse found a new rock bottom to lay and rot at. Anton and Vince, they'd gotten... *attached.* They opened up, and suddenly, I wasn't just a toy for them to exploit, a living sex doll. No, I had become part of the group, though not a part with freedom, like they had. I haven't left this mansion in four years, but they started asking me things, wanting my input on a new device, a victim, sometimes even giving me the option to say no when they wanted to fuck. Still, the illusion of a choice was more painful than none at all. I found myself disgustingly grateful for Jax's cruelty, because in all my fame and success, in all our time together, I was the cunt.

"I knew you'd look amazing in this. I had it made especially for you, Lana," Anton whispers against my neck, my body tensing at his touch. The tang of bourbon on his breath tells me he's going to expect more from me tonight, a proper show. He's always harder to please when he's drinking, which is a lot these days.

I'd rather be called cunt. Hearing my name from their lips is so much worse. That name is special; someone who loved me gave me that name. It being spoken in a place like this dirties it, ruins what little I hold of who I was before. I glance down at my feet, arched higher than natural in my sky-high heels. When my eyes hit the branded bit of flesh on my thigh, I avert my eyes. Among all the things done to me here, being marked like cattle was my least favorite. They'd carved their names into a circle on my thigh with a wood burner. For a moment, I wonder what their father would say if he knew, if he was aware of his billionaire sons' lucrative side hustle.

The Sullivans come from a long line of old money. Oil, naturally. The three brothers never did anything for themselves except this, a little business venture they'd started two years before they met Lewis and loaned him money, even though they knew he'd never be able to pay them back.

There's not much sexy or scary about kids born with silver spoons up their asses, endless bank accounts, and bone rattling boredom. Vince told me one night that they'd first seen a snuff film in their father's office, a VHS one of his bodyguards had taken the liberty of making, featuring another oil tycoon's six-year-old daughter. The way his eyes darkened and his cock hardened against me made vomit rise in my throat.

Vince watches me from behind the camera, setting up the stream, and my fist tightens on the speculum I had grabbed when we entered the room. The man's throat tearing screams play like background music in the room. I hate it when they wake them up too early.

Anton is still holding onto me, his heavy arms draped over my shoulders as he nestles into my neck like a child would with his mother. That's what Anton likes, the mommy thing. It's what he calls out to me as he ruts into me, whimpering like a child. My throat tightens when I think about that first night, when they came into the cold, concrete room we stand in now. By the time they left, they'd killed a part of me I had saved for someone who I loved deeply, a person I hadn't met yet but knew I would one day. I never doubted it, not for a second.

"One minute," Jax announces from the sofa set up behind the camera and large, pull-out projector screen they like to watch from.

"How many?" Anton asks, finally releasing me so I can get ready.

"One hundred and seventy-two...no, seventy-six. Mostly regulars, a few new faces."

I pull on the PPE gloves, grateful they got the longer ones this time. Our last trial run of this scene was around a year ago, a custom request from a longtime watcher, and I ended up being splashed by the acid. It scarred my lower arms, despite how quickly Vince rushed me into the bathroom to wash it off. The stuff works fast.

I can't breathe past the nodule of excitement budding in my chest. I don't know when it went from disgust to curiosity to downright excitement for me. I hated it at every stage, and the excitement doesn't make it any easier afterwards. They didn't permit me any stimulation for the first year—no books, TV, games, nothing. I was allowed to eat, bathe, murder, and spread my legs.

My frown deepens, pushing me to enter the scene early, and Jax's forced husky voice chimes in as always: "Who pissed off the cunt today?"

Anton chuckles at his stupid little joke, ever the obedient follower.

At some point, I was grateful for the walk down to the basement. Their unwanted touches were welcomed reprieves from the nothingness of that room. It took a little less than a year for them to move me up from their cells in the basement. It was more comfortable to rape on a California King bed than a dirty cot in the corner of a dark room. Anton and Vince acted like it was a favor, one they expected me to reciprocate constantly.

"Ten seconds," Vince announces.

The man bucks against his restraints, his ass tugged high into the air, bare and spread as he begs. Three years ago, I begged too. Three years ago, he and I weren't much different. Three years ago, I still hadn't accepted that I would never be more than the disgusting monster they'd made me. I'd never see Mom's smiling face again or know how Lewis was doing. That revelation was somewhat recent, and it still tastes like shit in my mouth.

"Live in five..."

"Four."

"Three."

"Two."

"One."

I run my hand down the man's spine, feeling him tremble beneath my palm, none of my usual giggling or twirling around. He's begging again, or maybe he never stopped. He lets out a heady sob when I remove my hands from his spine, reaching over to coat my fingers in the spit that's rolling down his chin, spewing from between swollen, red painted lips. I never really understood the lipstick thing, but funders usually pay more for it.

"Please. Please. I have a family, for fuck's sake!"

So did I.

He starts to wail, and my anger gets the best of me. I'm not angry with him, of course. He can't help his cries any more than I can help what I'm about to do. Some days, I feel more...bitter than others. My mind wanders as I round the table he's strapped to, the side of his face pressed into the metal surface, the stained wood of the rigging keeping his ass presented to the room.

I make a show of slapping his ass, each movement grand and exaggerated before working his puckered hole open. I know what's expected of me. When his cock inflates despite the horror he must be feeling, Anton bursts out laughing, earning him a smack to the back of the head. It's involuntary, but somehow, it makes this feel worse, more... disgusting. Again, my anger edges my self-control, pushing and pushing as I pause to glare over at Anton. What could possibly be funny about this? There's no excitement anymore, just bitter, never-ending frustration. I'm going to get in trouble if I end it too soon. I just...I don't have it in me today.

The speculum doesn't go in easily, but they don't want it to. I try my best to hide my wince as he screams despite me working him up to it. He's already tearing. I step aside, showing off my hard work to the camera, picturing all the nasty basement dwellers pumping their tiny dicks to my little horror show.

My patience finally hits its limit, the bitterness choking me as Anton gives me an approving nod from behind the camera. When I finally lift the jug of acid, I go entirely off script. No drizzling it along his back, no making him taste it, none of my usual showmanship, punishment and privileges be dammed. At least I know Vince won't let Jax take my books. That's all I really need. I tilt the container and watch as the clear liquid works down the funnel spout, sliding inside the speculum's opening. His bottom is opened wide, ready for me. I know the instant the acid hits; the man starts making sounds I've only ever heard from animals. When the gallon glugs, I can barely hear it, ignoring the top view camera winding closer for a POV shot.

Please, just pass out.

My guilt grips me quicker than usual, my stomach churning more with each of his frantic wails for help.

"I'm sorry," I whisper under my breath as his ass is filled to capacity, brown and red bubbling flesh working its way back up the funnel. It pops, and the smell makes my dinner curdle. The man's gasps trail off as his body goes slack in the rigging. At some point, those screams had been traded for vomit and a mouth gaped in agony. My breathing comes out roughly as I face the camera, giving them my signature curtsy, slamming the jug down on the cart.

I avoid Jax's furious glare, anger and disapproval rolling off him in droves. My heels clack loudly as I rip off the gloves, my hands shaking when I jerk the painted mask from my face. Its pretty princess features used to freak me out, like the expensive porcelain dolls Mom collects, but those dolls aren't stained like this is. The double doors slap back together behind me as I bow over, glaring at the floor, waiting for the vomit that doesn't come anymore, that hasn't in a while.

The clatter of the mask echoes in the opulent hall as I'm shoved against the wall. I'd hiss at the flare of pain from my back shaming into the molding, but Jax's forearm is shoved against my throat. "The fuck was that?"

Panic grips me beneath the surface, my body remembering the all too familiar sensation of being deprived of air. I don't fight back; I know better. Lifting my arms, I gesture to my throat. Jax's brown eyes track the movement, his light brows knitting together like the brain-dead asshole he is.

He doesn't make a move until he's satisfied, until my face is the desirable shade of purplish red. When he finally moves, it's with a shove, making sure to press extra hard. I don't get half a breath in before his hand grips my chin roughly, dragging my face towards his, repeating his question.

"Lazy day at the office?" I croak. Being a smartass won't get me anywhere, but since I'm already in the trenches…

The sound of his hand connecting with my face hits me before the sting of his palm, my head slamming to the side from the force of the blow just as his brothers join our little hallway pep talk. They don't intervene; they won't until it gets too bad. At one point, I might've even been able to dilute myself into thinking their infatuation with me might've been something more, something special.

It isn't.

Nobody likes to play with broken toys.

His hand connects roughly again. This time, it brings a familiar ringing to my ears as I sag against the wall. My higher-than-life heels slide out from underneath me as I sink down, the fancy dark molding scratching up my back before my mostly bare ass connects with the floor.

"You're going to cost us fucking money all because of a goddamn pissy mood?" he barks down at me before turning on his watchful brothers. "She's your cunt. What the fuck was that?"

I don't pick myself up; I know better. Being small is one of the few things that keeps his *corrective* slaps from becoming closed fists. I study the lines in the hallway runner instead, my eyes following every little swirl and leaf in the design. My fists are shaking, the burn of my nails digging into my palm not touching the throbbing in my cheek, but I know better than to touch that, too.

They're still arguing above me when Vince kneels at my side, brushing my red hair over my shoulder. "Lana."

"I have cramps," I offer, hoping he'll just leave it alone, take my weak excuse and go.

He rolls his dark eyes, ignoring the fighting of his brothers. "You're on birth control."

There're so many colors in this rug; I never noticed before.

I wince as his fingers prod my swelling cheek, forcing me to face him. When he leans in, his lips brushing past mine, the sick feeling in my gut roils.

"Vince, go get her changed. I think the Blood Princess has forgotten her place." Jax nearly coos.

Anton sidesteps, putting himself closer to me. "She's not leaving the house. It's too risky." I'm half shocked Anton spoke up at all, even as Jax's screaming cuts him off.

"She's a fucking tool here, not your goddamn girlfriend! Go upstairs, call one of the whores, and stay the fuck out of my way. I made her what she is. If it wasn't for me, the two of you would be inviting the cunt to family dinners and writing her little love letters."

Jax eyes are wide with anger when they turn towards me, his broad shoulders heaving in tune with Anton's as I finally work myself to a stand.

Vince's hands are hovering on the small of my back before his arm bands around my waist, tugging me closer. "She can handle it, Anton."

"Handle what?" I breathe out, working the stiffness from my jaw.

"You've had it too comfy here, forgotten your purpose, your place. Just because you keep my brothers' cocks wet doesn't mean you don't have to do your job."

"This is fucking bullshit," Anton spits before stalking off down the hall, his bulked muscles pulling underneath his shirt. He's the oldest of the brothers, the largest, but he always bows under Jax. He's just as cruel as his middle brother. If Anton isn't down for something, it can't be good.

"He's just scared someone will take you from us, Lana. You're a highly sought after item," Vince offers.

It's crazy how quickly my bitterness is drowned out by anxiety. My place here is far from good, but I know how much worse it could be.

"Just fucking—" Another slap cuts off my words, forcing a whimper from my throat as Vince catches me, keeping me on my feet. He's the…nicest of the three, usually levelheaded. If he's pissed enough to punish me, there must've been a high-profile watcher today.

"See, Cunt, our usual girls are… indisposed at the moment, meaning someone has an outstanding order for a handsome, fit, dark-haired man. You just delivered an unsatisfactory show. It's only fair you have a hand in fixing your fucking mistake."

My mouth goes dry as my hair is pulled taut by Vince. It's gentle, but that doesn't make it any less degrading as he forces me to face his brother.

"I don't pick the victims." My voice is softer than I've heard it in months, dread building inside me. *I can't.*

"Today you do. Perhaps the Blood Princess will think twice about wasting lives if she's responsible for choosing the next one."

"No, I-I can't pick them. Your girls go get them and I—"

"Sit on your fucking cunt in designer lingerie and read books all day while my brothers pump your ass full of cum!" Jax roars, spit flying from his lips. "You belong in the fucking basement, don't forget that!"

I try to wrench my hair free from Vince's hold, but it doesn't budge. My skull is on full display for the next hit. When the copper taste of blood fills my mouth, I choke back a scream. Not for help, or mercy, but because it would feel so good to scream, to release just a fraction of the fucking anger building inside me.

Vince lets my head go, keeping me pinned to his chest. His dark eyes find mine the instant I make a very dumb decision. Vince may be the youngest, but he's the smartest, the fastest. He likes to chase, and I found out the hard way that the more I ran, the harder he fucked me, the more he wanted it. He sees it the moment I decide to spit, his hand snapping my head down, my glob of spit and blood landing in front of his brother's shoes instead of in his face.

"Lana, enough," he snaps.

"When? When will it be enough?" Sweat prickles my forehead; I didn't mean to say it out loud. I really didn't. Questions like that only ever bring painful answers. I worked hard to get to the place where feelings rarely touched me.

"I'll handle it from here, Jax."

"You'd fuckin better. I'm this close to killing the cunt. Get her dressed and have her in the car in an hour. Get someone to put some fucking makeup on her face or something."

The chill from the basement is long gone as my skin flushes with heat. "Vince—"

He hushes me as he jerks me up, finally tearing my eyes from the bloody spit on the floor. I don't fight him when he bands his hand around my wrist, leading me down the long hall towards the staircase. Jax has long stomped away, but it does nothing to cool my insides.

When I speak again, we're far enough away that he doesn't stop me. "Vince, I can't have anything to do with picking the people. I can't stomach the idea of it." Two more stairways, and the door to my room looms closer and closer before he speaks.

"Four years making snuff films, and the guilt still bothers you?"

"This is different."

I can talk to Vince. I can make him understand. Anton won't let me out of the house, not even for walks. I don't want-

He takes a deep breath as he opens my door, ushering me inside, and my stomach drops when I see Anton lounging on my bed. He's glaring at the rich, draped canopy when he speaks.

"Why do you push him like this, Lana?"

"Anton, please, talk to—"

"If you so much as think about running while you're gone, I promise you, Lana, I will make sure your junkie brother suffers a fate worse than yours. Do you understand?"

The light delusion I had convinced myself of on the walk up here shatters abruptly, taking with it the ever-evasive rage that had been bubbling in my chest. The mention of Lewis reduces what seconds before was an inferno, waiting to erupt, to embers.

My breath escapes me all at once as Vince gives me a warning squeeze. "Yes. I understand." How could I have forgotten? This isn't about me; it isn't about what *I* can handle.

I'm the breeze.

Anton shoves up from the bed, stalking over to where his brother has already started undoing the lace back of my lingerie. "There's our girl," he chuckles. "As much as I wish you'd stop pissing him off, it's fucking hot watching you get all worked up."

I don't make a sound when Vince slips my lingerie off my shoulders. "We need to get you dressed; he's waiting."

I don't breathe when Anton captures my face, forcing a heady kiss. The press of flesh on flesh makes my bloody, swollen lips throb. His tongue assaults my mouth, the taste of blood whiskey souring my already curdled gut.

I'm the breeze.

2
Hunting

I let my mind drift as I drive, Jax's hand resting on my lap, his fingers making small circles in the jeans they found for me. *My* jeans. I haven't worn real clothes in years; they fit me far looser than before.

I always thought I'd feel more comfortable covered, but I'm not. Vince and Anton prefer to keep me naked or dolled up in lace. My wrinkled university t-shirt is musty after years of being shoved in some closet, I'm sure. I nearly gasped when I saw it. Jax's hand gives me a little squeeze, a warning, the metaphorical gun pointed at my head. He hasn't ever fucked me for pleasure, for fun like his brothers. He reserves his cock for punishment, and I try not to look as it presses against the zipper of his pants. I think of my brother instead.

The time I caught him sneaking out of the house to go an after party for the carnival that was in town. He begged me not to tell Mom, his eyes wide and hands clasped together like he was praying. He only stopped after I pinky promised, only to lay out an entire directory of reasons why we should both go. It was the most fun I'd ever had in my life. I was jealous, though, undeniably so. Lewis never let himself be weighed down by consequences, responsibility, or anxieties. No, he just lived. He laughed and danced and did body shots off a man who had body modifications to make himself look like a lizard. He was sixteen. There sat his eighteen-year-old sister on a dusty arena bleacher, laughing and giggling at his antics, but I sat alone. It was the most fun

I'd ever had because it was the most fun *he'd* ever had. At that time, at least.

Anton leans up from where he was scowling in the backseat to offer me a drink from his flask. I take it greedily, anything to calm the torrent of nerves in my gut. "Jax, you should get back here. We're about to hit the city."

"I—"

"You'll drive until you see a bar or a man. Dark hair, handsome. Shouldn't be too hard for a pretty cunt like you."

Yeah sure; other than the fact that the sun is setting, and I haven't driven in four years with near night blindness. Oh, and I haven't spoken to anyone other than the Sullivan brothers in what feels like a lifetime. I don't even remember how to be normal… how to flirt or not be … *her*, the side of me they built on tears and vomit. Oh, and blood. So much blood.

My palms are slick with sweat. Thankfully, neither of my companions or the other two muscular men for hire say a word about me constantly wiping them on my pants. The music on the stereo makes it even more difficult to focus on the road, the lights of businesses taunting me with the illusion of normalcy. When it starts to rain, my pulse thuds so loudly, I can hear it whooshing in my ears.

"Hey, scout car said there was a guy stranded up ahead," one of the men hidden in the back of the large SUV pipes up, making me jump. Four on one seems like overkill, but then again, everything with these guys is. Why Jax didn't just make me go with the normal trained team has me on edge. It feels like foreplay.

When the outline of a car comes into view, I swallow hard. "Shit."

"Well, look at that. Seems God hand delivered him to you," Anton chimes in. "If that's not fate…"

The car up ahead is nice, too nice to be having car trouble in the rain at nine o'clock at night. I can see a tall figure walking around it, the hood up, smoke leaking from somewhere. I certainly can't tell if he's hot or not.

"Fuck this up, and—"

"I get it," I cut Jax off, knowing this is one of the few times I'll ever get away with it as they all duck below the seats.

The SUV rolls up, the stretch of road I now vaguely recognize. The city we're coming up on is the one I lived in. Nerves flutter inside my stomach as I pull behind the car, my breath refusing to do anything but leave my mouth in rough pants.

You're not Lana. It's no different without the stupid costume.

We couldn't have been driving for more than an hour once they pulled over and forced me to get behind the wheel. Another twenty minutes, and I could be home.

I could see Mom and Lewis.

The rain is cold, the way it always is in the fall, like maybe, just maybe, we could get an early dusting of snow, an unexpected frost to kill off what's left of the flowers. When he steps around the raised hood of the car, my lips part. His white, button-up shirt is soaked from the rain, his short dark hair dripping, the fabric molding to his sculpted chest and arms like you'd see in a painting.

"Uh, hi."

Yes, brilliant.

He nods, his deep green eyes sliding over to the SUV for a moment too long. My heart slams into my chest as he studies the vehicle. "Any chance you know a lot about cars?" he offers, tilting his head as he looks back down at me.

My words are lodged in my throat as he steps closer. Holy shit, he's hot. Deathly so. His dark black hair is cut short, the waves giving way to curls. Everything about him screams money, screams that he's not someone who can just go missing from the side of the road without consequences.

"No, can't say I do. Sorry, I, uhm..."

The closer he comes to me, the further I step back towards the SUV, every single fiber of my being urging me to get back in and drive away.

"Were hopefully about to offer me a ride?" He smirks, his voice a deep tenor that matches his devilish looks.

I almost say no, I really do.

"Yeah, it's a shit night to be stranded out here. The city is pretty close."

He chuckles, running a heavily tattooed hand through his wet hair. "Missed it by that much, huh?"

I force a laugh of my own, my fists shaking as I dig them into the pockets of my low waisted jeans. "Does the wet and mysterious stranger have a name? You know, in case I need to report you for being a creep later." I don't know why I ask, or why I watch him so closely as he closes the hood of his car, at the way his muscles move underneath the fabric, flexing and pulling.

I never know their names. She doesn't care about them.

But Lana did, at one point. I used to collect them on a piece of paper folded and stuck to the back of my vanity with toothpaste. I would tell their families one day... I'd atone.

"Christian." He chuckles, closing the distance between us with a lethal grace. "What should I call you, princess?"

My footing slips, sending me slipping down the ditch. Frigid and immediate panic grips me like a noose around my neck as he lunges forward, catching my arm before I hit the ground.

"What?" I gape. My panic is so pungent, my teeth chatter loudly in my skull.

"Sorry, not a fan of nicknames?"

Right.

I shoot him a weak smile as he helps me back up the ditch. "Princess suits me."

The truth behind those words sink straight to my bones, taking the edge off the panic. *Princess* does suit me, mask or not. I'm her. He's alone, just another body, just another scream, another trickle of blood, another step closer to keeping my family safe. "Let's get out of the rain before I break something."

I never could put a visual to the phrase "his smile darkened" before, despite reading it constantly in my books. Still, I can't think of a better way to describe what his face just did, the warmth bleeding into something else as he wrenches open my door, rushing me in.

My breathing is loud, louder than the radio, even as I watch him walk round to the passenger side in all his handsome glory. He's perfect, checks all the requested boxes, but there's an unease in my gut. Gone is the casual charm and panty wetting smirks. Suddenly, it's not me who's taking him.

It's him who's taking me.

Part of me, a larger part than I care to admit, wishes he could.

My hands are shaky, and his eyes aren't missing a thing as I drive. They roam over my now-damp and musty clothes like they can see what's underneath, like they've memorized every curve before.

The backseat?

Deathly silent.

Until it isn't.

A scream tears from my throat as Jax and Anton lunge up, the sound of four guns cocking in unison filling the cab, all of them trained on Christian beside me.

"Shame, you really thought you were getting a piece of our girl, didn't you?" Anton spits. Out of the brothers, he's the only one who ever shows any jealousy when it comes to me, always needing reassurance he's my favorite.

My chest heaves as I pull over again, quickly backing out and turning the SUV around, heading not towards the city, to freedom, but to the gates of hell itself.

"Hey, I—" Christian starts, only to be cut off by the barrel of a gun being driven into his skull.

My stomach lurches at the sound, my foot instinctively slamming on the accelerator, making the tires spin on wet pavement.

"Who fucking taught the cunt to drive?" Jax comments about the time I risk a glance at my hostage.

He's all tension, those dark green eyes trained not ahead but on me. He doesn't cower, no begging or tears. He's still, those Greek God-like muscles tense and ready. My head snaps away the moment our eyes meet.

"Give me that shit!" Anton curses, the fumbling from the backseat only egging on my nerves.

The cap of a syringe is jerked off as I barrel down the road, and minutes after they stick him with whatever drug, I muster enough courage to look at him again. My stomach drops to the floorboard. Christian smirks at me as his body sags, the drunk, heady look you get from the handsy guy at the bar after you finally let him buy you that drink, a man who just got exactly what he wanted. It's gone when his head knocks against the dash roughly.

My voice is hoarse when I speak. "Guys, I don't think—"

"Shut the fuck up and pull over. You're driving like a crackhead," Jax cuts me off, and I'm all too happy to relinquish control of the vehicle.

When Anton pulls me into his arms, caging me in his bulk like a gorilla, I can't help but breathe easier for a moment. The last thing I ever thought I would find in the arms of a Sullivan brother is a sense of safety. The driver's door slams as Jax takes over, pulling back onto the road I'd only barely pulled off of before I leaped from the vehicle. For the rest of the ride, I let Anton pet me, and my eyes never leave the curly lump of hair attached to Christian's head.

3
Punishment

I count the grooves below me: one hundred and twenty-six so far. My fingers are numb as I work them open and closed from where they are tied over the bar above the table's suspension rigging in the basement. Forcing me to my tippy toes, Jax holding my hips so I'm kept at an angle. When my head lolls back, the lack of color in my hands tells me I won't be getting the feeling back in them anytime soon, my wrists tied to the bar tightly enough to bruise.

My teeth dig into my bottom lip, failing to bite back a whimper as Jax thrusts into my ass, the deep ripping burrowing into my stomach like sandpaper. I'm so dry, he has to force it in. The spit he used to work his cock in the first time has long since dried, and I doubt even he's getting much enjoyment out of it at this point. It's a small consolation knowing he's going to be raw tomorrow, too.

That is, until Christian stirs. The drugs they'd given him are wearing off earlier than I've seen them before. I glare at the table below, having lost count of its grooves as his moss-colored eyes flutter open, the disorientation quickly blinked out as another cry is forced from me. Another thing taken I didn't willingly give. Making me weak in front of a victim is new. It feels like shit; the indignation it brings is quickly stomped out as Jax leans against my back, sinking his teeth into my shoulder.

I scream.

I can give them my screams.

Not my tears.

Christian strains against his restraints. I imagine by now that he's painfully aware of how badly I fucked him over. Maybe he'll get some sense of justice watching this. The gag in his mouth muffles words I can't focus on right now. Blood is already pooling, gathering in the indents Jax's teeth left behind, my dry, tight hole ripping with every thrust. Humiliation hits me for the first time in years.

I'm the Blood Princess.

I inflict.

Nobody is usually around to watch karma take its ounce of flesh.

Anton glares from the couch, all of us ignoring the thrashing of Christian—

The victim.

I won't meet his eyes. I can't share in my shame, or the Sullivan brothers will get something they don't deserve.

My tears.

Vince never stays when Jax takes me. I've never understood why. He's not jealous like Anton. He's his own breed of cruel, just without the audience.

"Fucking little bitch, stupid fucking cunt. Doesn't deserve my cock."

I try to force my eyes to settle again on the grooves underneath him, fighting the urge to look directly at the man strapped to the table the upper part of my body is sagging over. Instead, they find a dark birthmark on his stomach, just above his black boxers. I almost smile; it looks like a cumulonimbus cloud, the type that comes before heavy rain. I love rain almost as much as clouds. I started school to become a meteorologist not too long before everything changed.

I know the moment some kind of unique damage has been done when suddenly my asshole gives, and the dry forced thrusts become slick. My knees finally buckle, gut wrenching pain barreling up my spine, the kind that makes my teeth score my lip hard enough to puncture the already damaged flesh.

"...fucking your bloody asshole, you fucking..."

Cumulonimbus clouds can reach heights of up to sixty thousand feet, making them the tallest of all cloud types.

The man jerks on his loosening restraints in my peripheral, and I wait to see if anyone will notice. They don't.

"...make you shit on my cock..."

Cumulonimbus clouds are associated with extreme weather, heavy downpours, hails storms, and even tornadoes.

The man is cursing, but I can barely hear him now. The pain consumes everything as my soul is once again ripped from my body, taken, abused, and then shoved back into a place it no longer belongs.

Individual cumulonimbus clouds will usually dissipate within an hour once the rain starts, making for powerful but short-lived storms.

Nothing at all like a summer breeze.

When my eyes open again, it's to Vince's body pressing against mine, taking the weight of me as he undoes my restraints. The man has stilled as I'm lifted into Vince's arms, and my eyes find Jax. He gives me a nod before tugging his shirt off, using it to wipe off his blood and, to my horror, shit slicked dick. All the while, Anton bitches at him like a spoiled child who was just told to relinquish their favorite toy.

I let myself melt into Vince for a moment. It's these...the times where I need him that he wants the most. Vince is just as terrible as his brothers, but in a quiet way, the way that feeds off me being so thoroughly damaged, I need to be nursed back to health by *him*. My head lolls back as I'm carried from the basement, my eyes accidentally meeting a pair of deep green ones. What I see there is far from the fear I'm used to. It's rage, a promise... a fucking vow. I shudder, using the last of my strength to bury my face in Vince's shoulder.

The water stings as I'm lowered into it, the warm bath filled with expensive oils easing the worst of my aches as Vince runs a smokey gray loofa over my bruising flesh. His thick brows furrow as he passes the bite mark, his long, dark hair falling into his face.

Vince doesn't like it when they bite me. That's his thing.

He bites hard, over and over until my flesh looks like one of the neglected potholed back roads of my city.

"You need to control yourself around Jax, Lana," he admonishes.

Because I'm the problem.

I just nod, leaning back before sinking underneath the water, wishing maybe, just maybe, the hand he's using to wash my chest will press down, taking away my choice to resurface.

He doesn't, and eventually, my lungs demand it. I pop from the water with a gasp, my eyes burning from the oils they like to bathe me in. It's probably their mothers' tears or something like that. Vince hums to me softly as he forces me to my knees in the tub, forgoing the loofa to clean my ass with his bare hand.

A strangled sound leaves my throat, the pain making my hands shake. His touch is far from delicate, but it's welcome compared to Jax as he parts my cheeks and prods at the damage. I do my best to ignore the blood tinging the water. He stops cleaning me only long enough to feed me his cock.

I choke on his length, my red hair pulled taut in his fist as he stuffs himself deeper than my body wants to allow. My nose is stuffy from the cold rain, and each inhale is forced, making a whistling sound as I'm forced to swallow him. Tears prickle in my eyes as he holds me there, unmoving, his dark eyes gazing down at me with something akin to admiration. It's the way you'd stare at your prized racehorse after it broke its leg on the track.

Seconds before you put a bullet in its skull.

My hands squeak against the edge of the tub as I grip it, my knuckles popping with the effort to hold me still. When he finally moves, backing out of my throat, the breath I drag in is ragged. Anton discards the plate of food he'd walked in with at some point, the sound of his buckle nearly drowned out by my coughing.

The bruises on my face throb in tune with everything else as Vince grasps my chin, forcing me to look at him. "You're going to make tonight up to us, right, Lana?"

Dread pools in my belly as Anton makes his way behind me, inspecting the damage.

"She can't take you like that," Vince snaps, roughly jerking me from the warm water, crashing my body into his clothes. I can't help but flinch. Vince is cool, like an ice storm, and every bit as deadly. His rage comes all at once with an unhinged lethality I've only seen a few times.

That was enough.

Anton whistles. "Damn, baby, he really tore you up this time."

"Wow, I hadn't realized."

Vince smirks, finally releasing me from his chest, his chipped black nail polish shining as he snakes his hand down my front. Deft, well-practiced fingers find my clit, and I focus on the pink-tinged water, the way the bubbles swirl as he thrums. It feels better with Vince than with his brothers. Somehow, that has always made it worse. At least Jax doesn't want me to enjoy it. Anton just wants me to pretend to, but Vince...he can tell the difference. He won't stop until my body relents, forcing more from me, the betrayal of myself.

Anton takes up station behind me, shoving his cock against my hand until I take it.

This time, when I relax into Vince, it's not some harlequin knight in shining armor I picture, with his rippling muscles, long blonde hair, and azure blue eyes. This time, as my belly tenses, my hips rolling in tune with his fingers, despite the painful tug in my ass, the knight has moss green eyes, dark wet hair. It drips onto my face as he teases my clit in tight circles, stopping to run his long fingers up my slit, teasing but never pushing in. His white button-up shirt is clinging to him, molding to every groove, letting me glimpse the expanse of tattoos underneath.

"Fuck, Lana," Anton moans, now content to use my hand as a pocket pussy.

Christian watches me intently as my lips skim his jaw, my tongue darting out to taste him. Vince's moan almost ruins it until Christian pulls me back, his free hand tweaking and pulling at my nipple.

"I need you," I whisper, giving myself over to the fantasy. When that tight line bursts within me, it's not the gentle release of pressure: it's an explosion. I'm lost to it, carried away by the blast. I don't feel the ropes of cum hitting my back as I bite down on Christian's shoulder, moaning and whimpering so loud, it echoes in the large bathroom.

All too soon, the waves pass, Christian's hands replaced by Vinces as he gently—too gently—removes my head and teeth from his shoulder, forcing my face towards his. What I see there in his dark brown eyes is wrong. His hand raises, prodding the angry, raised flesh.

His eyes never leave mine and they're *wrong*.

So terribly wrong.

"Leave us," he growls.

Anton bristles at my back where he'd been rubbing his cum into my skin. "No, I want to dress her. You did it—"

Whatever look Vince flashes him is enough, and Anton storms out of the room with a slew of curses. I can't focus on a single one because now, I'm panting. When Vince directs his forehead against mine, ice floods my veins. When his lips touch mine, I die inside.

He kisses me for the first time, his lips deceptively soft and... needy.

"I- I need you too, Lana."

Oh fucking hell.

4
Stream

I avoid Vince's eyes like the plague as he braids my bright red hair down my back, my face looking even more sad and gaunt than usual, though maybe it's just the deepening bruises. This time, when Anton enters, I pull free from his brother, fleeing whatever new connection Vince thinks formed between us. I don't fight Anton as he gathers me up in his wide arms, holding me up like a child.

"I'm too tired tonight. Can we please—"

"You know Jax isn't gonna go for that, baby," Anton admonishes. "Buyer is already waiting on stream."

My heart drops further. "A private viewing?"

He nods, eyeing my braid and then his brother with no little amount of disdain. When Vince steps towards my wardrobe, Anton roughly discards me on my bed. "I'm dressing her."

I can't stop the hiss of pain when my ass hits the pillowy mattress. My stomach lurches as I roll to my side, fighting the urge to cry out. That need doubles when Vince appears at my side, caressing my back.

"What the fuck has gotten into you, Vince? We fucking share her!"

"Why?" he retorts, his voice quiet, calm, but his hands tighten painfully against my skin.

"What did you just fucking say?"

I'm still on the bed, my eyes darting between the brothers, the tension in the room thick enough to suffocate.

"We can talk about it later." Vince whispers, leaning down to press a kiss to my temple. "Put her in black."

"Damn right we're talking later, and I'll put her in whatever the fuck I want." I cringe at the sound of the wire hangers sliding around on the metal bar of my wardrobe. "Better not let Jax see you kissing on her like that." He half laughs, letting the tension dissipate enough for me to release the breath I was holding. "He already thinks we're pussy whipped."

I wince as Vince spreads my cheeks, looking again at the damage there, his dark eyes dipping a shade or two. Out of the blue, he gives a fuck, all because I was a little too responsive. I gave him the validation he'd apparently been waiting for. How long? God, how many signs had I missed?

My teeth dig into my bottom lip as Anton jerks me off the bed, pulling my towel away. He's not gentle, even by his standards. He's acting as if this is my fault, like I want his psycho brothers' affection, like I wanted to fantasize about the man downstairs. No, Jax *had* to make a point. I *had* to help. He *had* to be devastatingly handsome, handsome enough to take the place of my knight in shining armor, and now?

Now, I have to kill him.

This one is different; my family's safety rides on this performance. Earlier was a mistake, one Lewis and Mom can't afford. I'll do my job, and everything will go back to normal. I can go back to ignoring all three of them, and Vince can get that fucking look out of his eyes.

This time, when they lead me down towards the basement, I'm ready. I'm ready long before they hand me the mask.

Christian

<u>Self Destruction by I Prevail</u>

My eyes finally leave the crater sized hole I'm glaring in the back of Jax Sullivan's shaved head as the heavy doors to the chilled room burst open. From where I'm *mostly* tied down, I can't see the dark metal, nor can I see her when she walks in, but I know she's here all the same. My fists tighten in my restraints as the picture of her face pitched in pain floods my mind. I'd never seen her face before today, but I know her well.

The Blood Princess. A legend in the flesh. She's tiny without that mask, delicate, breakable. I wanted to break her when I let her lead me to her SUV, knowing what was waiting inside. My palms ached with the need to break her. Seems these fucks beat me to it.

Vince Sullivan's hand is plastered to the small of her back, and I decide to kill him second. Jax first, obviously. The semi sheer mini skirt and corset top she's wearing molds to her perfectly, fitting her like a glove. Her mask is already in place, but now that I've seen underneath the porcelain princess mask, I'll never forget it. Her amber eyes find me immediately, her chest hitching as I keep her attention. I shouldn't be able to see her, but oh, I can. I'll never *stop* seeing her. She's why I'm here, after all. The Sullivan brothers may be old money, but they're new blood, and there's no room for new blood in my world, a world my family has dominated for generations.

Snuff.

New blood makes mistakes, like picking up the guy stranded on the side of the road less than an hour from their secluded mansion. New blood doesn't ask questions, or the new blood would've realized the fucking mistake they made. Sure, my car breaking down was an accident, but my being there, so close to their home base, was anything but. What's the line that curly headed painter used to say?

Happy little accidents.

I test the left restraint, the one that's clasp I jerked apart, the muscles in my arm shaking from going on four hours of being held up with nothing to support its weight. Another new blood mistake: never keep them up and sober, always check the restraints.

Then check them again.

My heart drums in my chest as my little princess twirls in front of the camera, her mini skirt flipping up to show the light coating of blood between the round globes of her ass. My teeth clack together hard enough to make my jaw ache, and my skin prickles as I feel someone's eyes on me, regrettably not hers as she plays in front of the camera. Vince Sullivan is leaning on the far wall behind the screen, his dark eyes glaring at me with the same vigor as I glared at his brother, and now him. There's no real reason to pretend to be scared; I'm already here. What they mistook for my panic earlier is still simmering in my chest, a rage I haven't felt in years. I couldn't get free, couldn't risk it, not when there was so much at stake.

My eyes don't leave his, something close to bitter malice shining in them, and it almost makes me smirk. Perhaps he's just as pissed about the way his cocksucker of a brother handled my princess. I bet he even thinks she's his. The anger in my chest sizzles up my throat, burning, razing my insides until it demands release. Vindication. She's not his. She hasn't been since the moment my family decided to take her.

The moment I saw her face, she became more than the rival's cash cow.

She became mine.

Mine.

The fuck's eyes widen a fraction, but it's already too late. He shifts uncomfortably, balling his hands into fists. Hands that haven't seen a day's work. Hands that have no idea what true brutality is.

My princess walks towards me, her wide hips not as plump as they were in older streams. Her arms are smaller too, her hair not as shiny—all things that can be fixed. It's the light hiss she lets free as she leans down, making a show of picking from a line of tools, that needles into my skin, my first warning of things to come. Sure, she's mine—mine to fuck until I'm tired of it, mine to exploit—but that doesn't account for the bizarre concern I feel. She's in pain, yet they force her to perform. It's clear what happened earlier was a punishment, a bad one. Not even the prick drilling into her managed to get off from it.

She leans in close, that pretty doll mask turning as she slowly pulls and tugs my wet clothes away from my skin. I breathe deeply, sucking in the warm amber smell that's coming from her. It's deep and sweet, and it fits her perfectly, like candied fruit. The blade wizzes quickly across my stomach, cutting my shirt down the middle, and behind that mask, her breath hitches.

Do you like what you see, princess? Look lower, there's more for you.

I strain my fingers, capturing a loose strand of hair as she moves closer. Her hair is soft like silk. Behind the mask, I can feel her perusal. She's taking me in, *drinking* me in. My eyes finally turn from her long enough to gauge what she chose for me. It's a modified blade, some gear attached to the handle.

For a moment, I wonder if I could take it, wishing I had more time to watch her like this. It'll be the last time from the victim's perspective. Fuck, it's heady. She winces as she climbs onto the stained wooden table, standing over me, giving me the loveliest view, even if it is a little bloody. Blood never bothered me.

She steps back further. If I wasn't playing victim, I would applaud her balancing on the wide table in her heels. She takes each step carefully, with grace. I should stop her from removing my pants. Fighting is much easier with them on, but I don't want to deny her an eyeful of my cock if she wants one.

She pauses as she eyes my hard length straining against my pants, dropping to a squat over my knees. Her fingers brush out, feather light, caressing the head, and I have to bite my inner cheek to suppress my moan. Those raw, swollen lips would feel like heaven spread over it. When she presses the bottom lever, activating the spinning blade, it jerks me back into focus. Foreplay is over when my lust clears and I realize she intends to split my dick lengthwise and not tickle it again. The room erupts into chaos the moment my hand leaves its restraint. First, it's from Vince Sullivan, who shoves off the wall, the beginning of what sounds like a girl's name on his lips.

Jax intercepts the sick fuck eager to see what I'll do to her as she cries out, losing her balance. My shoulder flares in pain as I jerk out, snatching the blade from her chilled fingers. It takes me less than a second to let my momentum and weight crash back down, the blade whirling as I cut through the other leather restraint on my hand.

Vince is still fighting with his brother, but Anton is free. Only a second more hesitation, and he decides to intervene. "Cut the feed!"

It's a second too long. My princess lurches for another weapon from the table, this time a hatchet, swinging it down in a wide arc, but her angle is off. Its tip barely nicks my shoulder before I snag her by the throat, pulling her into my chest. She's warm against my damp, cold skin, and my fist smashes the modified blade against the table, jamming the control lever into the *on* position before I throw it, a sick smile growing on my face as it lodges in Anton Sullivan's neck. The princess in my arms is thrashing, crying out for... *them*.

After everything.

My smile dissipates quickly as I wrap my arm around her neck, ignoring her claws as I use her hand still on the hatchet to chop through the restraints at my legs. The remaining brothers, to their credit, react fast, but not fast enough.

5
Taken

Freak on a Leash by Korn

*L*ana

Oh God, oh my God.

Panic and maybe a little vomit claw up my throat as I scream. Blood is still spewing from Antons's neck as the man all but drags me off the table with him. All my kicking, wiggling, and scratching seem to be no more than a minor inconvenience to him, despite the feeling of his skin and blood building underneath my nails.

He's going to kill me.

God, please kill them too.

Get them all.

If that was in slow motion, everything next occurs in hyper speed. Christian jerks me behind him, ensuring his is body towering over mine as Jax's voice rings out over the chaos, and with it, the sound of a gun cocking. *Two* guns.

He's not holding me now, but it's not any easier to draw air through my lungs. Oh God, Lewis. I'll never see Mom or Lewis again. I always knew that was likely the case, but now, with panic overwhelming my senses, it's all too real. Tears spring into my eyes as Vince's dark form creeps around behind Christian, still far enough away to stay out of the man's reach.

Vince's eyes are hard but worried as he jerks his head, ordering me to walk away from the man. I take a step, a tiny one, but my feet won't listen. Fuck, my body won't listen. I can feel the tacky blood between my legs as Christian's back presses against mine.

Jax will punish me for this. I know it.

"Two guns against one unarmed man. Those aren't good odds," Jax snips.

I take another step backwards, closer to the stranger. *He* notices, his arm coming back ever so slightly, tugging me closer as he twirls something in his hand that I can't see.

"I don't know, Jax. I quite like my odds." Whatever I picked up to kill him with, maybe. My mask is lopsided on my head, my hands trembling as I reach up to tug it off.

"How the fuck you know my name?"

Vince's eyes dart to Christian's arm where it cages me against his back. "Lana, come here," he orders.

I can't.

Can I?

"Take a step, princess, and I kill you too." Christian's voice chills me, goosebumps breaking out over my skin.

"Lana!" Vince booms. My entire body wants to collapse in at the sound. I've never heard him so loud. His gun isn't pointed at the floor anymore—it's pointed at *me*. "Come here. Let's not forget what you stand to lose. You don't know him. You're ours, Lana."

I'm the breeze. How could I forget? Only, what's a summer breeze in the face of so many storms? I crane my neck, getting a lungful of Christian's aftershave as I look towards Anton's body. The sight of him bloody on the floor doesn't fill me with the immediate relief I thought it would. My breath shudders from my lungs as self-preservation, for the first time in years, forces me into action.

My heel clacks loudly against the floor as I lurch away from Christian—not towards Vince, but the overturned cart. My knees scrape along the rough concrete as a once eerily calm room erupts into chaos again. A shot rings out, and in the reinforced bunker they use as their kill room, it's deafening. My hand grasps the only thing close enough. Ironically enough, it's the jug of acid. More shots rattle my brain, and I'm only vaguely aware of Vince gaining on me as I rip the cap open, throwing the entire jug at him.

I'm leaving.

I'm going to go home.

Vince screams as the jug makes contact with his chest, the liquid inside splashing up into his face as his finger squeezes the trigger. I don't take a moment to check on him, or to see if I got shot. If I did, I certainly don't feel it as adrenaline floods my veins. The familiar sound of an unyielding object impacting flesh filters past the ringing in my ears, a sickening, wet thud.

I hiccup, my eyes blurring with tears as I scramble for Vince's gun, my hand stopping seconds before I would've maimed myself. Acid covers it and everything near him, and the jug glugs as he screeches, wildly wiping at his face, taking skin with it. If I were Lana, I might feel bad. I might even help him like he helped me that day, but I'm not Lana. Not yet.

I scramble to my feet, darting around the center rigging as a warm substance splashes my face. I scream, waiting for the agonizing burn, but it doesn't come. When I finally stop wiping my face, my eyes drop to my bloody palms. The slopping sound of object versus flesh breaks me from my ill-timed panic. Christian is standing over Jax, his muscular form splattered in blood as he delivers another hit of Jax's gun against his skull. My eyes dart to the door, everything screaming to leave, leave before anyone else comes. The room is soundproof, but the video was live. Sooner than later, someone *will* come.

It's Jax's groan that stops me. "Lana," he croaks, reaching out to me with a bloody, shaky hand, slumped a few feet from his brother.

Lana?

I'm not Lana.

I stare at him as he groans again, his face a misshapen garble of features. I don't look away; I don't run, even though the door is right there. My way out is right there, but I'm stuck, staring at Jax there on the floor. Christian jerks down Jax's pants, smirking proudly as he flips him onto his stomach, jerking his ass in the air. My gut swirls, and I stay...enraptured as Jax whimpers. He fucking *whimpers*.

For Lana.

How many times did I whimper before I finally stopped?

My knees threaten to buckle underneath me, so I shift my weight again, feeling the tackiness between my legs, fresh blood from my ass mingling with coagulated.

Blood freckles Christian's handsome face, and he pants as he angles the gun, pressing it between Jax's cheeks. Jax buckles and fights, but it's weak, the sour smell of his vomit filling the room as he tries to drag himself away. "Lana!"

"I'm not Lana," I whisper.

Christian turns towards me, keeping up with Jax's very slow pace. Those mossy eyes bore into mine for so long, I forget to breathe. It isn't until Christian tilts his head towards Jax before I realize he's waiting for me. My throat goes dry, my bloody knees wobbling as I shake my head.

"Lana, hit the button!"

"I'm not Lana. I'm the cunt," I whisper again.

Christian shrugs to himself. "We warned you to back off."

Jax screams as Christian forces the barrel of the gun, slick with blood, into his ass. "The Vanegas family sends their regards."

Jax lets out another bloodcurdling scream.

Vanegas...

I've heard Jax bitching about them, the empty threats they made against the brothers for cornering the snuff market. The Sullivan streams all but robbed them of their viewers the moment I came into the picture.

Vanegas...

My stomach lurches as my brain knits together the information.

"Lana!" Jax roars as Christian fucks him with the gun. He rams it into him, burying and wiggling it deeper in the same violent, unyielding way I was taken earlier.

Christian chuckles. "The name is Christian, silly, Christian Vanegas, and the princess is no longer your concern. Now, tell me, Jax, are you going to shit on your own gun?"

Like a whip, I'm released from my spot, throwing the heavy doors open as I bolt into the hallway. Vince's and Jax's screams pop into the hall for a moment, and I barely catch the sound of the first gunshot. I'm barreling down the hall towards the exit when the doors open again, not giving a single fuck if I'm seen by the few staff or guards that stay on the grounds. I'm halfway through the arched kitchen doorway when my braid is yanked back roughly, sending me colliding into Christian's wall of a chest.

"Now, now, princess, let's not get ahead of ourselves."

I open my mouth to scream before his hand clams around it, hugging me tightly to his chest as he tucks us inside the large pantry. His warm breath tickles my ear as he leans in to whisper, his lips teasing my neck. "Hush now. We have company."

My struggling ceases as I watch a pair of shoes, the stubby heels all the housekeepers wear, prod through, the shadow coming in from underneath the opening to our side. It's open, wide open. All she needs to do is look up from the fucking cart. I open my mouth to bite down on him as she passes, headphones over her ears as she bobs her head along to music I can't hear.

"What kind of contingency plan is in place for you should they all die? Do you think they'll release you, princess?" he whispers. His cock is hard against my back, and panic rears inside me again as he shifts. I squirm, fighting him again until he gives me a warning squeeze, tight enough to abruptly end my breathing. He shifts his hips back, keeping his sizable junk off my ass.

He knows it hurts...

"Perhaps you can stay in the mansion, keep up the streams without the Sullivans."

My chest heaves, silva coating his hand from my ragged breathing as he eases us from the pantry, navigating the house as if he's lived here for years. The muzzle of the gun is still hot as it finds my back, and my eyes dart to the knife block as we pass it. My neck is wrenched back at an ungodly angle as I strain against his hold to grasp one. The second I do, I plunge it into his back. The familiar pressure of meeting flesh comes only a second before his grunt; Christian releases me for a moment, and it's all the time I need.

His gravelly voice comes like an omen, a warning. "If you run, I will chase you, and if I chase you, I'll make you regret running, princess!

My sweaty palms slip on the handle of the back door as I fumble with the locks. The door flying open fills me with an obscene and unwarranted degree of hope as I bolt through the backyard, headed for the woods, for the access road that runs to an old trail Anton said they used to ride bikes on.

A woman's scream billows from the house and next, the ear-splitting alarm. The following flurry of gunshots only add to the erratic beating of my heart. I don't waste a second looking back as I run, my chest heaving, my lungs burning already. I used to love running, but I haven't run in years, and it shows.

My bolt through the woods is long, and the early morning light does little to illuminate my path. Again and again, my steps falter, my brain offering what if.

What if I'm going the wrong way?
What if I should've stayed?
What if they aren't dead?

I sob when I see the opening of the trail ahead, tears again bursting in my eyes. "Lewis, Mom!" I don't why I scream for them, but I do. God, I do, and it feels so good. I scream again, finding that once I start, I can't stop. I'm screaming, only taking enough of a break to sob or force my lungs full of air. But the hope, like always, is short-lived.

One of my heels snaps off, sending me careening toward the ground. A searing pain shoots up my calf from my ankle as I fumble with the straps to peel them off. My own breathing nearly drowns out the sound of boots pounding against the trail behind me. I scramble to my feet, ignoring the blasting pain as I run. I'm not fast enough. God, I'm not fast enough.

Christian gains on me quickly, blood pouring from his abdomen. When my heel trips me again, I don't miss the satisfied look on his face.

"Please!" I yell, scrambling back as he slows to a walk. Soon, his tall frame, the shadow of him, eclipses me on the ground. It's not a physical one, but his very being shadows me in a way I've never experienced.

I watch as he lifts the gun. "Sorry, princess." His shitty apology is the last thing I hear before he brings it down on my head.

6
Placement

*C*hristian

My princess is still out cold by the time I made it back to my car, and I jerk my cell phone from the glove compartment. The pain from her various attacks on me really starting to put a damper on things. As expected, the torrent of texts and missed calls annoy the absolute fuck out of me as they come in volleys, the overpriced modern technology struggling to keep up with the wrecking ball force of my family. I ignore them, opting to call Kallen instead.

My eyes follow the trickle of blood as it weaves a new path down her forehead, my frown deepening as I count every bruise on her delicate face now washed clean from the heavy makeup that caked it earlier. I had imagined what lay under the mask countless times out of sheer boredom or horniness, but I'd never gotten close. The idea alone of something so delicate being capable of such intense cruelty has my dick springing to life.

The Blood Princess, a legend who dominated the snuff world in less than a year, consumed it entirely in the four she was active. The woman is personally responsible for five hundred and three deaths of the most unhinged nature. Watchers empty their life savings for a spot on her docket, a ticket to the show. The Vanegas family, known online as Venance Vanegas, went from the top dog to the half dead one you buy from the pound because the owner guilt tripped you into it.

"Christian? Your father has—"

"I'm sending you my location. Bring a car and," I glare at my car, "probably a tow truck, a mechanic. Just get here and ensure Dr. Lamaison is on standby at the compound."

"Sir..."

"Don't inform my family—"

"Jesse is standing in front of me, sir."

"You are a ball sucking cuckold, Kallen."

I hang up, sending my encrypted location his way before again shutting off my phone. The princess, *Lana*, groans in my arms as I awkwardly lower myself half into the passenger seat, rooting around in the center console for something. Her pretty, honey-colored eyes flutter open the second I plunge the needle into her upper arm, and her gasp lodges in her throat as she tries to lurch from my grip. My arms tighten around her hand, knocking the needle from mine, and I scowl as it flips through the early morning air down the embankment, every thrash adding to the throb and burn of my wounds.

Her full lips gape, and I can feel her scream before she forms it. I clasp my hand over her mouth. "Can't have you drawing attention to yourself."

She doubles down on drawing attention to herself.

Her elbow connects roughly with the underside of my chin, giving her just enough time to wiggle worm free from my arms. She stumbles, like she wasn't ready for the weight of her own body, as she bolts for the road. The throbbing in my chin is no more than an annoyance as I watch her head back in the direction of the mansion. Based on all the trials I ran, the Sullivans pay-to-play security is just as lackluster as it was all the other times I set off the alarm in the past few months: nowhere to be seen. Even then, I can't risk her meltdown.

She's panting down the middle of the desolate highway, her steps already growing uneven. I can see her breath in the chilled air, the shaking in her limbs. Her red braid could barely be considered one at this point. Her rounded ass jiggles as she stumbles, righting herself by sheer luck as she fights gravity. The drugs are quickly taking their effect; I didn't account for her loss of weight. I don't chase her down, tackle her or stop her attempt to flee. It's much more interesting watching her hobble away from me. She just keeps going, her corseted breasts heaving with each pant. She knows I'm behind her now, close enough to reach out and touch her goose bump adorned skin. To lean down and lick it if I had the time to.

I decide to make time.

My mouth waters at the thought, my hair falling into my face as I lean forward, my tongue darting out to capture a bead of the sweat on the back of her slender neck.

"Lewis." She whimpers, her knees finally giving out from underneath her.

I swear I meant to let her hit the roadway; I really did.
But I caught her instead.
I also swear I'm unbothered by the unfamiliar name on her lips.
Entirely unfucking bothered.

Her pretty wide eyes flutter as I grip her chin, forcing her face towards mine. "The name is Christian princess. I'll let that little slip up go this time considering your current condition."

She makes a sleepy, indignant noise in the back of her throat, right before she spits on me.

I wait for the rage, for my fingers to let loose their hold on her chin and slip towards her neck. I wait for the overwhelming desire to throttle the ever-loving piss out of her. My cock jerks instead. She's fighting the drugs, her eyes fluttering closed only to be snapped open again. So delicate and small cradled into my chest; her legs bent underneath her in a kneel. I release her chin to wipe at the spit on my face, promptly licking my fingers free from it.

She shudders, this time not fighting it when she closes her eyes, I pry her full lips apart. Giving her spit back to her, and a little of mine. She cries out, gagging on my fingers just as a pair of headlights illuminate behind us.

Her teeth score my fingers as I withdraw them, her head lolling as she finally succumbs. My muscles strain as I clutch her. Deciding with direction is the quickest to make it back to the weapons in my car without having to release my hold on her.

"Sir!"

LED headlights nearly blind me as Kallen's huge frame jumps out of the rolling SUV. Three others from the trail car following suit. My body is wrought with tenson and exhaustion, my groan loud as I stand. Shooting daggers at the nameless fuck that seems all too ready to wrench her from my arms, "Attempt to remove something from my arms that I have not offered to you again and I'll crack open your fucking skull and send the video to your mother."

He bristles, his eyes taking her in before giving me a curt nod. "Sir."

I decide to definitely do that, later.

After a nap.

A very long nap.

Oh, and after I wring my dick for being an insufferable twat all night long.

7
Gilded

Lana

Lewis laughs like a madman as he repositions his twin sized mattress on the stairway. I give my obligatory big sister *don't Lewis. Mom is going to be pissed.*

Which he promptly ignores.

His squeal of delight warms my chest, snuffing out any lingering annoyance at the mess I know I'll mostly be cleaning up this evening. His long shaggy hair blows past him as he bombs down the stairs, the tip of the mattress hitting the lip of a step a little too soon. Our twin laughter cuts off in unison as he flips forward, the glass screen door making a death shudder as his head collides with it. I barely register the sound of his phone hitting the floor as I dart down them. My heart ratcheting in my chest. "Lewis!"

My hands flutter all around him like panicked little moths as he groans, canting his head backwards. "Please tell me you got that on the video."

My eyes widen, dumbstruck as blood pools in his hairline. "Oh, my god you're bleeding. Mom is going to kill us. Are you okay? Don't- don't move."

He rolls his eyes, which makes him groan again as he rights himself shoving the mattress off him where it landed. Lewis' hands clap on either side of my cheeks with a gentle smack, "Lana. Did. You. Get. That. on. Camera?"

I frown, glancing up at the phone on the landing. "Probably not?"

"Dammit, you had one job!"

My frown turns to him. "One, don't curse. Two, you can't afford any more brain damage, so forgive me for not being concerned about the video!"

I almost laugh as he raises his knees, burying his head between his legs, stringing along about how his friends are going to think he's full of shit.

I punch his arm gently, letting myself laugh now that I know he's not too badly hurt, but still my heart is racing. My hands shaky.

When his warm eyes turn towards me, my stomach free falls. His face is older, haggard, a deep pock mark on his chin. Vomit surges up my throat at the terror in his eyes, the shame. Suddenly we aren't in the sunny hallway of our childhood home. The muggy night air wraps round me. The smell of burning oil, sweat and blood.

The Sullivan brothers close in, and when their hands touch me this time, I'm not crying silently, reassuring Lewis with a broken voice that I'll be okay. This time, when they shove me in their expensive car, I scream.

My eyes fly open, only for me to shut them again. So tightly colors begin to kaleidoscope behind my lids. My sheets cling to the sweat sheeting my body as I press myself back into them. Ignoring how gross it feels, the uncomfortable stiffness in my body. It's been years since I slept through the night. The only indication of morning is the warmth of the sun I can feel pressing into my sore flesh. Of all the nights I spent with the Sullivan brothers, the first was by far the worst.

It was a first for so many things.

I lost my virginity that night. I don't even remember who took it. Probably Jax.

They replayed the video of them beating and taunting Lewis at full volume as they took turns with me on the cold basement floor. It smelled so strongly of bleach it made my eyes burn. My chest, knees and back were so bruised they swelled painfully from the force of each of them mounting and flipping. Slapping, beating and choking. Eventually my throat bled from the force of my screams, they didn't stop. When I finally stopped crying, stopped reacting to anything they were doing, they didn't stop. My heart raced from the blow they forced up my nose, but I was numb all over. It started the brutal loop I lived in for the first year. Rapidly going from completely shut down to feeling everything all at once.

They broke me that night.

They made me forget about the breeze.

Shuffling in the corner of the room doesn't alarm me. I rarely wake up alone. I do my best to lie still, maybe... maybe if they think I'm still asleep, I can stay in bed. Preferably without a cock in me. Maybe I can even read a little before I'm forced to follow Anton and Vince around all day. I hold no purpose unless I'm being fucked or performing, so in the down time I simply... *exist* in their space. I'm not expected to clean, cook, fold, or bathe myself. Not allowed anything but my books and pretty lingerie to try on. New shipments come in almost every day. Sometimes they want me to model with new rigging, sometimes I was a guinea pig for something non-lethal until Vince put a stop to that.

Long minutes pass before I relent, deciding it's better to get the day over with than drag it out. When I open my eyes, I'm groggy. The canopy above my bed is gone, as are all the rich tones and wood. What greets me is sleek, modern, and minimalist. The world has suddenly gone from technicolor to black and white, and with it comes painful clarity.

The man moves closer, and I press my legs together tightly, wondering if I release my overfull bladder, he'll hold off on raping me. When the smell of deep, masculine aftershave hits me, I roll my head towards Christian. All my bravery in the end didn't do shit to change my circumstances, only the tower I'm kept in.

"Good afternoon, Princess."

Christian

Her fiery hair is fanned across my gray sheets, the parts underneath her dotted darker from her sweat.

She doesn't offer me any pleasantries, which is a little rude but understandable, considering her position. My phone rings loudly, interrupting our staring match. I pretend to pull it up, watching her in my peripheral as she tentatively releases the sheets, snaking her hand down to prod at her sex, seeing if she's been fucked.

I school my features against my smirk. Unconscious girls aren't my thing.

Just as I say that, my eyes land on the overflowing wastebasket of cum-filled tissues in the corner, from when I stood over the Blood Princess, jerking my cock like I just hit puberty off and on for the last twelve hours. Her brows furrow as she feels the thick pad placed in her new underwear.

"Would you have preferred I let your ass bleed all over the bedding?"

She doesn't respond, her cheeks flushing a pretty color.

I wait for her answer, eyebrows raised, but when her teeth dig into her bottom lip, I realize she doesn't feel like she's allowed to, a dangerous status quo to break if she's a talker. I can't stand meaningless conversations.

A growl slips through my lips as my phone rings again, jerking it to my ear. "What?"

"She up yet? You've been up there for a while. No fucking around until she's—" Jesse barks into the phone, barely taking a breath before I interrupt him.

"No." I don't know why I lie.

"Fuck. How much of that shit did Doc give her? He said ten hours tops."

I hear rustling on the other end before Father's voice takes up space here my younger brother's had been. "She's got a few more hours to wake before I send in Dr. Lamaison to push the matter. The sooner she's lucid, the sooner she can be brought to terms with her new situation. We want minimal disruptions before the announcement. The watchers are already getting wind of something going down with the Blood Princess streams. Luca hacked and tore down the servers, but it's only a matter of time. We need her performing at peak before people start making claims of a takedown."

I don't answer, my eyes trained on my princess as she stares at me, the same numb resolution I saw in her eyes as that fucker took her ass. My phone case creaks as my grip tightens.

"....and son?"

"Yes?" I snap a little too loudly.

"Get her the fuck out of your wing." He ends the call just as abruptly as he hijacked it, par for the course with the head of the Vanegas family. Irritation flares in me, because he's fucking right. She shouldn't be here, and she's still looking at me like that, the way she looked at them. It's pissing me off. Any comparison to Sullivan filth would, I suppose.

That's what I tell myself.

Their money is in the real world, fed to them by daddy dearest. They had no place down here. At least the Vanegas don't pretend to be upstanding citizens, good, ivy league cunts. We've always been clear about what side of the law we stood on. Snuff, drugs, and guns were our claim to fame long before her.

Before *her*, their little videos were laughable. Then, things went dark. A small fry got tired of seeing no pay off in a high-risk world and blinked out before the heat turned into an inferno.

She works her throat again, now avoiding my eyes, looking around for something. A wince follows every swallow. I could show her where to get the water, but the idea of her leaving my bed makes me want to wrap my hands around her throat. I could get it *for* her. I can't name a time I served anyone anything other than death or pain.

I give her my back.

After things went dark with the shoddy Sullivan streams, they came back, like a nasty cough. Suddenly, the production was better, the little clips turning into full length streams overnight. From her very first one, people were hooked.

I swipe the iced thermos of water from behind me, pouring her some in a small paper cup. She sits up immediately, wincing as she goes. Her little pink tongue darts out, desperately wetting her lips, and I fight the smirk that pulls at my face, my cock already growing at the idea of her needing something only *I* can provide.

I drink the water.

I don't know why I do it. I have no reason to be a fuck to her and every reason to make her as comfortable as I can. We want her on our side. Killing her is also an option, but talent like that shouldn't be thrown away.

I fill the cup again, waiting.

Ask me, princess. Ask me for a drink, and I'll give it to you.

"Were you there against your will the entire time, or did you just have a change of heart halfway through?" It doesn't matter to me either way, but we're building rapport. Stolen help is new here, especially of the snuff variety, but we aren't barbarians. You catch more flies with honey than vinegar.

Why I've decided I'm the most equipped to build rapport who the fuck knows. She doesn't answer, but she does eye the cup. Her nipples poke out from underneath the sheets like diamonds, begging to be rubbed across my lips.

"So you really were having as much fun as it appeared on camera."

It's bullshit. I'm positive, even before Dr. Lamaison relayed the mile-long list of injuries she sustained over the years. Fractures that never healed right, chemical burns down her arms, her x-rays lighting up like Whoville on Christmas night. None of it was as bad as the vaginal exam—seems that was the only place they were willing to purposely scar her. Even my father winced when the doctor talked about her ass. My fists clench, the paper cup crumbling in my palm, forcing the icy water out over the edges.

She stares at the liquid dripping over my fingers like a kid would after you drop-kicked an ice cream cone from their hands, sucking the fucking fun right out of it.

I mumble a slew of curse words under my breath as I get a new cup, all but shoving it at her. She doesn't hesitate, drinking it down greedily. A trickle of water slips from the corner of her mouth, trailing over her gentle jawbone and down her neck, begging to be licked up. All of it, everything, annoys me. Unsettles me.

Nothing about this woman is sharp, nothing edged out. It's all gentle curves and swells.

I refill her cup, handing it back to her.

I'm not acting like myself, much less the second in command of one of the most feared crime families in the country. A family known for shit so atrocious, they don't even put us on the most wanted list. It's all tucked away, out of sight. Letting them take me had been a knee jerk reaction. I'd like to say it just looked too good to pass up, but no. It was the way she walked; the timidness didn't hide the grace I'd seen through the screen hundreds of times. She *slipped* in the mud. It was like watching a deity stumble.

She was so... soft.

Years of tracking, stalking, and planning, and I let them take me.

To get to her.

"The doctor said you need to stay off your feet for a few days." She just frowns at her empty cup, and I fight the urge to refill it. "He also said there's a stool softener he can give you to make your... other issue more manageable." The words leave me stunted, anger making it harder to choke them out.

I know immediately the second she mistakes my reluctance to mutter them for disgust. "I've managed this long without meds," she snaps, unexpected venom filling her warm eyes.

I think my heart palpitates.

Hello, princess.

Her cheeks flush deeper, but even a fuck like me can't take much enjoyment in her embarrassment, not about this. When the need to reassure her claws up my throat, I nearly vomit, growling out a *fine* before stalking from my bedroom. The door slams behind me, the full bizarreness of my actions settling in.

I just fled *my* bedroom to avoid a woman *I* kidnaped.

My phone rings again, and I promptly hurl it at the wall, watching the pieces burst apart before falling to the hardwood floor. I pace, working out frame by frame the exact moment I became obsessed with the Blood Princess.

8
Flux

Lana

I wince as I slowly lower myself onto the floor of the large shower in the attached bathroom, my ass throbbing as it presses against the floor. I didn't ask for permission, only answered the burning need to scrub away my own humiliation and pee. He kidnapped me, drugged me, and had a doctor examine my lady bits.

It says a lot that only the latter has me glaring holes in the tile floor.

Domineering, hotter than the gods, voice like liquid velvet *Christian* knows that I have poopy problems.

Fucking swell.

My fists clench, and I can't for the life of me understand why I even care. I certainly never did when the issues started, never so much as blinked an eye when Vince realized something was wrong, then Anton. I only found out Jax knew when he started making fun of me. His new goal was to ensure my ass was entirely unusable. I'd rooted for him. Maybe then, I would die of sepsis, an impacted bowel, or something entirely lame like that. I certainly didn't need a doctor to know that the manner in which I was taken there had messed things up quite a bit. Even just feeling around myself could've told me the scar tissue was in the way of, well, *everything*.

The water is hot as it beats at my back, the near painful power washer setting bordering on uncomfortable, but I don't care enough to try to figure out the control panel. In those early days with the Sullivans, I didn't have permission to even turn on a light, let alone mess with their shower settings.

A quick glimpse around the moody, cluttered bedroom told me it was occupied. Not just a spare I was chucked into.

It smells like him.

My embarrassment flares again, making me groan. I'd just sat there stupidly, irrationally mortified for a full ten minutes after he stormed out, until that too was boarding on painful. I knew better than to even try the damn door, opting for the bathroom instead. After I peed, a quick glimpse in the mirror better sealed my horror.

Again, why do you care that you look like fresh shit?

Maybe because, whether he knows it or not, Christian saved me. More importantly, Christian saved Lewis. No matter how bad it got here, with whatever intention he has for me for, however long.

He saved Lewis.

No more brothers left to threaten him. No more Jax, Vince, and Anton.

No more fucking Jax.

If I'm lucky, which I'm not...

No more Blood Princess.

I almost cry at the incredulousness of that thought, as if I'd have been worth taking for any other reason. A strange sob like sound leaves my throat, and I'm not sure if it's out of relief or fear. When it dissolves into manic laughter, I can't tell if it's because the totality of bullshit is kind of fucking hilarious, or if I've finally lost my goddamn mind. I'm laugh-sobbing so hard, my belly aches, my ass burning and throbbing, replaying Jax's whimpering over and over until the sound of someone clearing their throat stops me abruptly.

My eyes widen on the salt and peppered face in front of me, just now noticing I'd forgotten to close to the glass door, the puddled water on the floor reflecting the stern and entirely unamused man's face.

"Glad you're feeling well, Blood Princess. We need to talk." His voice bleeds authority. Maybe that's what freezes me in place, the sudden unknown after years with the brothers. I'd learned to expect the cruelty, could anticipate it a mile out. The same faces every day, staff who were never to interact with me. The brothers... as much as I hated them, I *knew* them.

He sighs, and I do my best not to cower—*I fail*—as he stalks over to me, wrenching me from the shower floor. Even after years spent with every sensitive part of me exposed for viewing, I'd forgotten what it feels like to be truly naked. My feet can't get traction as I try to fight his hold.

Stop fighting, Lana.

God, I can't. Panic jolts my heart into hyper-drive as I claw at his arm. When his hold on my slippery arm isn't good enough, he trades it for my hair. We're halfway out of the too large bathroom when I manage to twist in his grasp, kicking his knee from the side. He grunts, cursing, and I hit the ground. *Hard*. My hands fumble on the counter, finally grasping a heavy, decorative thing I can't even identify the purpose of. I lift it, my arms shaking. For a moment, I'm calm.

I'm her.

I can see what I want to do. I know how to do it. Maximum carnage. But the people I kill are rarely untethered, and even at his age, he's fast.

Faster than me.

I've been shot in the head.

There is a bullet currently lodged somewhere very important in my skull. It's the only logical reason for the stabbing pain currently obliterating my every thought. There are also... hands, roaming, prodding, and pushing, though willing my eyes to open does very little to make that happen.

A sharp prick, a burning sensation in the crease of my arm, makes me jerk slightly before that too sends the bullet racketing around inside my skull. Have you ever seen the bizarre things a human does when their brain becomes compromised? I once drilled into a man's skull Dahmer style. After I spent a moment or two poking and pinching, his cock inflated like a life raft, coming over and over until he sobbed and vomited, the appendage a choked shade of purple and blue.

It was one of my best steams. Jax was thrilled. Even I was a little fascinated by it all.

When warmth spreads from my chest to my belly, it rushes forward, making my already muddy thoughts slower. Slowly, I breathe easier, the pain subsiding bit by agonizing bit. Now, there are voices with the hands. I can't make out their words, nor can I tell if the voices only just showed up, or they've been here the entire time. Rubbing alcohol assaults my nose as some kind of bandage is pasted to my arm. I want to kiss whoever created the drug I was just given. It's oddly enough the loveliest I've felt in years. I was never allowed downers, only coke when I wasn't energetic enough for their liking.

There's a loud commotion. Despite the new unbothered state of being, it makes me flinch. My hands fist the thin blanket I'm covered by as the angry, loud voices turn to a struggle just outside of wherever I am.

A man screams, but it's cut short. I'm confident I could open my eyes now, run a triathlon even, albeit slowly, but I don't. The door somewhere close bangs open. "Where the fuck is she?"

Another scuffle, more grunts. Now, I'm holding my breath.

Christian asks the same question, at top volume, but the words are darker, more menacing than anything I've heard from him before. He's closer now, maybe even in front of the room.

"Sir should we lock—"

"No."

A shudder breaks out over my skin at the gravelly voice. Glimpses of me being pulled out of the shower by my hair makes panic ratchet in my chest, threatening to obliterate my high. Not a bullet, a fist. A heavy one. I've been punched before. God, I can't recall it ever hurting that bad.

The door to the room slams open, and I can feel him the moment he enters. His rage. It shouldn't comfort me—God knows it shouldn't comfort me—but it's better than the severe salt and pepper man sitting nearby.

The monster you know.

"You had no fucking—"

"Enough son."

Son. Son?

Christian lowers his voice, and somehow, it's scarier. "You had no right to enter my wing, much less my bedroom, and jerk my—"

His dad scoffs, but even that manages to sound refined. "Yours? We've had possession of the alleged Blood Princess for less than a full day, and already you've staked your claim. That's simple minded, even for Jesse, let alone you."

The smell of Christian assaults me, adding to the warmth. It's his aftershave mixed with sweat. It's heady, and my drug addled brain wants more. I think of the way I came in the bathtub, pretending Vince was him. When his dark eyes land on me, I can feel it, my cheeks flushing as if he somehow read my mind.

"Yes, it was after all our ineffective planning it a pure accident that landed her in our arms. It was *me* who killed the brothers. It was *me* who grabbed her. It's only logical she's *mine* to acclimate."

Another scoff from his father. "Acclimate? That's how you're trying to spin having her in your bedroom instead of the dozens of fully furnished staff rooms? Nothing is logical when one thinks with their cock. We ne—"

The other quiet man in the room clears his throat, shifting uncomfortably next to the bed. "Sir, I believe she is awake."

Well shit.

"Princess, it's impolite to eavesdrop," Christian admonishes, his velvet voice smoothing over my nerves before frying them again.

My eyes open reluctantly, just enough to take stock of the situation. Yes, I'm restrained to a bed, in a room with three men. The man standing by my head looks more interested in the tablet in his hands than what's going on around him. That's partly reassuring. Christian's father is seated in an aged recliner, a cane resting across the arms, his knee wrapped tightly in a brace. He's fucking terrifying, but it doesn't appear he wants to rape or beat me at the moment.

I drag in a lengthy breath, finally turning my gaze towards Christian. He's shirtless, painfully so, a pair of basketball style shorts doing close to absolutely nothing to hide his bulge. His hands are wrapped like boxers do, fisted at his sides as he glares down at me. My eyes linger on the scratches marring his rich skin, the bloody bandages on his shoulder and side. I can't meet his eyes, so I study the dusting of blood splatter mixed with his five o'clock shadow.

"How's her head? Can she understand us?" his dad asks, ignoring me.

Christian's head snaps towards him. "What happened to her head?"

Another man appears in the hall from behind them, every bit as handsome as Christian, but he has a boyish quality to him. He's grown, but at least slightly less bitter. His wavy, dirty blonde hair makes my heart wrench. He reminds me of Lewis, what Lewis could've grown into if he had never found drugs, if pock marks didn't mar his handsome face. The man leans casually in the doorway, his suit jacket looking out of place on him. "Before or after you pistol whipped her?"

Christian's words are more a growl than anything. "After."

The tablet guy seems to be getting tired of all the back and forth and steps in front of Christian, earning him a death stare. "Hello, my name is Dr. Lamaison. Are you in any pain?"

My eyes fall back to the man leaning in against the door. My chest aches, but not in any physical sense. I shake my head. Not even that I can feel.

The doctor nods. "Good. You have at least two—" he shoots an apprehensive look at Christian— "moderate concussions. With time and rest, you should feel better in a few days. As far as your other injuries, they are healing as expected. I have a lax—"

"No, thank you," I croak, my eyes slamming down to the bed.

I barely suppress a flinch as the doctor reaches out, gripping my hand tightly in his. "What you endured—"

"Don't. Touch. Her." It's a warning, one the doctor obeys. The venom in Christian's voice makes my skin break out in goosebumps. I can't tell if they're the good or bad kind.

The man behind them chuckles. "It's his fucking job to touch her."

"Not anymore."

With a heavy sigh, their father stands. If his knee hurts, he doesn't show it. That annoys me more than it should. "If that is all, you can send any imprudent results to me—"

Christian steps closer, damn near shouldering the doctor out of the way. "I will handle any medical—"

"Christian!" his father snaps. "Enough of this."

Christian ignores him, despite everything about the man commanding attention, his scuffed hands making quick work of the restrains on my ankles. I feel like a fly on the wall, but it's a conversation about me. Nothing new, but the unfamiliar faces make it more anxiety inducing than I'm used to.

Soon, Christian's large hands find my wrists, undoing the restraints there. Each pass of his fingers sends a thrill straight to my core. He'd done the same when I was performing, caressed me with the tips of his fingers. It unsettled me then, and now... it's far from unsettling. Like his father, Christian commands. His sharp features and strong, clenched jaw, the pissed off look in his eyes, scream *I just escaped from the back storeroom of an Abercrombie and Finch.*

My chest tightens, my teeth digging into my bottom lip.

"The Blood Princess was my task, and my sole purpose for the last year and a half was to find her. It only makes sense I would see it through." Christian voice is calm, reasonable, but his hand finds my ankle, tightening around it like a vice as he turns back to his father. It's a warning.

A dare to disagree with him.

The dirty blonde man whistles, his eyebrows so high, they damn near touch his hairline. If my assumption was that Christian's father wasn't someone you disobeyed, this confirms it. When the silence stretches on, the doctor nods curtly to the room and dips out, followed by the dirty blonde one.

My breath loges in my throat as the glaring match continues, each man radiating enough malice and authority to kill a baby elephant with a single look.

When the man's eyes shift from his son to me, Christian's hand tightens further, leaving bruises in their wake. His body is tense, ready. For what, I can do without knowing.

When his father speaks, it's the same brand of velvet as his son, but wiser, the cadence of someone who won't be rushed. "I assume you need little explanation of what will be expected of you here, but I will offer one anyway. You will stay here, perform when you are needed. You will be fed, clothed, no different from any other member of staff. You—"

"Did you kidnap all of your staff?" The words slip past my lips, the tension in the room forcing them from their hiding place beneath my tongue. If I'm to be held against my will again, I would rather familiarize myself with the monsters pulling my strings, and that includes figuring out just how little freedom I have.

"My staff are quite happy, the ones who don't owe me anything. If you comply—"

"*I* owe you nothing. Not streams, not loyalty. I am done with the Blood Princess. Let her die in that house with her *masters*. You get your monopoly back on the snuff industry, and she fades into the recess of the internet, where she should've stayed." I don't know where my confidence is coming from. Maybe it's the way I had again dared to hope, only for that hope to be obliterated. Maybe it's because, for the past four years, my every step has been chosen for me, my every moment filled with people I hated. Maybe it's Christian's hand on my ankle, the chain it represents. It could defiantly be the drugs. My stomach sours; I'm at the very beginning all over again. It's Jax, Vince, and Anton, only these men don't have that bargaining chip.

Lewis and Mom are safe, for now.

For now... I have a leverage I never had before.

Maybe I'm just fucking tired.

Too tired.

Maybe the breeze eventually stops blowing. Maybe it lets the summer sun, the storms, kill every last thing it ever cared about.

He smirks—if you can call it that—the slightest tilt of his lips skyward. "You have an opportunity here. A choice."

My laughter bursts from me, as cold and cynical as the blood in my veins. "I have *no* choice. I have never had a choice."

"They forced your hand, but the tides have changed. I'm offering you a position. You can take what they *forced* upon you and make it something that works *for* you. Or, *I* can force your hand. I assure you I am far more horrifying than that Sullivan scum."

I believe him.

I really do.

He seems fit to leave it at that for the moment, stalking from the room before he turns over his shoulder. "Christian, I will see you in my office this evening. She stays in this room, or I have her gutted, and the last year of your life was wasted obsessing over her for nothing."

It's funny the way a blade can be positioned at your throat for so long without you ever realizing it's there. My eyes find Christian as he glares forward, his sculpted chest heaving, his fist absently rubbing against his right thigh, a tick that betrays his façade. A year, huh? That's a long time to be searching for little ole me.

The thought settles in my gut like a lead weight.

9
Allies

Christian

I tried to leave her alone because, logically, I should. I should leave my father, maybe even Jesse, to beat, bribe, talk, or fuck her into submission. The server's eyes widen on me as I hold out my hands, demanding the tray of dinner. Her dry skin cracks as she grips the edges of the tray harder. "Sir, I was told to see to it personally that she eats."

Apparently, the last two days I've spent snapping at everyone, boxing until my body threw in the towel, and jerking my cock raw, she hasn't. What point she's trying to make by being hungry is beyond me.

"And that worked so well for you the last *six* trips you made down here?"

Not that I've been counting.

Her mouth opens, my suit jacket already too tight for me today. The laces on my shoes came untied once. I spilled my coffee. My new phone won't stop ringing, and it's everyone's fault. I'm on edge, because of my—*the princess.*

A very stubborn, hungry princess who refuses to accept the inevitable. She will take up the mantle we made for her; she'll serve until she can no longer. Then, she will be killed. Not much different from her situations with the Sullivans. The guards might even take a liking to her. My chest grows hot at the thought of their hands on her, wondering what sweet sounds she'd make.

Lana, Lana, Lana. You're becoming more of a liability than a fucking asset.

The younger girl nibbles at her raw bottom lip, and. I do my best not to threaten to kill or maim her. She's a timid thing—no family, no friends outside of the trade she was kidnapped into when my father bought her from a brothel in New Orleans. Said she looked like my sister, Abigale, but I don't see it. She can stay here, earn a wage, get her health and mind in order, the same deal offered to my princess.

Not yours, Christian. Not. Yours.

Only difference being, *the* princess cannot leave. She knows it. Nobody does what she does, as well as she does, and gets a chance at a happily ever after. *A normal life*. The girl finally relents, handing me the tray before quickly bolting back up the stairs. Father always had a thing for strays, cats, dogs, *people*. I never understood it. Why hire reformed whores and murderers, druggies, and people broken beyond help to do the cleaning when you could find someone with less baggage? The girl's sobs echo off the wide, empty halls.

I stalk towards her room, making the food under the domed platter jostle, probably spilling on the inside. My eyes scan past the open security station, the guard inside picking his nose in front of the dozens of screens. Before I can consider pausing and demanding a new one, I punch the code into the locked door, breezing through it.

Her head snaps up towards me, her eyes resolved. The gray sweats she's wearing are a far cry from the designer lingerie I'm used to seeing her in. Even so, she's fucking stunning, the same way a small, rare bird is made even more so because it would be so easy to kill it, so easy to have it stuffed, to keep its beauty for yourself. Her red hair is braided down her back, the same way it was the night I took her, the strands unraveling since she's not allowed any band to keep it together.

The room is clinical, small, devoid of anything to help pass the time, only containing a bed, recliner, and desk. The bathroom attached is barely big enough for the shower inside it. She crosses her legs underneath her as she fiddles with a frayed hem on the blanket.

I just stand there, food in hand, staring at her like a dumbfuck, trying to figure out what to say. And *as* I stand here like a cuck, people upstairs are busting through the few files we managed to pirate from the Sullivan servers before the wall slammed back up. Not a great sign, considering there should be nobody left to give a fuck. Unless this is their daddy's version of a clean-up job, but even that makes little sense. Why leave it open versus just wiping the evidence entirely?

Soon enough, I won't need the princess to divulge. I'll have any information we could possibly need. Still, it doesn't stop my palms from aching with the desire to pry all her secrets from her pretty lips. I shift on my feet, gripping the tray harder than necessary. Irritation flares inside me as she goes back to focusing on the blanket. Her eyes should be on me. Endlessly. I want her attention; I *need* it. For a moment, I'm a fucking child, standing quietly in a full room, begging to be noticed. It's pissing me off.

"I told the girl I wasn't interested in eating," she offers finally.

Very well.

I sit the plate down in front of her on the bed, tossing the lid off. The metal makes an unholy sound as it bounces off the cold tile floor, skidding to a stop. To her credit, she doesn't budge. I lift the packet of oyster crackers right in front of her eyes. "You like these? Never saw the purpose of them myself."

She just stares at the crackers.

God, give me fucking strength.

I deposit them in the soup we had for dinner, stirring, grateful most of it stayed in the bowl. It's what they've been putting her stool softener, vitamins, and antibiotics in, like a fucking toddler. A woman I once watched bust a man's testicles under her boot like grapes, then force a woman to lick it up, seconds before she buried an axe in her back...is being tricked into taking medicine like a stubborn three-year-old. And me? The feared eldest son of the Vanegas family, a man who has lived thirty-seven years and most of them spent killing, torturing, and ending lives, is blowing on her soup.

So it doesn't burn her fucking mouth.

What in the holy mother of fucking hell is going on right now?

She stares at me like I've just asked her to recite Shakespeare backwards as I lift it to her mouth, offering it to her. "Either you eat yourself, or they call the good doctor and force it."

She doesn't open her mouth.

Okay, I tried.

I jerk my gun out of my waistband, flicking off the safety and pulling back the hammer in one fluid motion. "Say ahhhh."

Her eyes flick towards the gun pressed against her forehead, then back at the spoon before opening her mouth. She doesn't look worried about the gun. In fact, she doesn't even glance at it again. Several more bites, and I start to lower it. She looks almost concerned as I do, like she doesn't know what to do without it. She doesn't know what to do with the choice, the kindness. I doubt they gave her a choice in anything.

Noted, the princess responds to violence, but it doesn't scare her. Find out what scares the Blood Princess.

Part of me hates that, more so than the fact that they had her figured out in a way I don't. The other part, my cock, is already straining against my zipper. She takes another bite, another bite that

I feed her. It's a sick kind of satisfaction, and I school my features to pretend I'm not getting off on it. We sit in silence as I offer her bite after bite, and she takes them, being so deceptively *good*. My cock strains until every throb is painful, a wet spot forming on the crotch of my three-piece suit.

When the bowl is empty, the soggy oyster crackers left at the bottom, I reach for the rice, my princess shakes her head. "I'm full."

My hand tightens around the small bowl, my eyes darting around the room, searching for a reason to argue, any fucking reason to stay in here for a while longer. Why? Because apparently, I'm a fucking masochist.

"Christian…" she hesitates, drawing in an unsteady breath "Are they all dead? You're positive?"

I damn near see red. Here I am, debating on force feeding her lukewarm rice just to spend another ten minutes with her, and she's thinking about the fucking Sullivan brothers.

My hand finally releases the small bowl as I slide the tray onto her desk. I don't answer her right away, shifting back further on the small lumpy bed so my back hits the wall. She shifts closer, her small hands reaching towards me, and I nearly stop breathing.

"You don't understand—" She cuts off, those pretty golden eyes shining with tears she won't let loose. Her hand is paused, caught between neutrality and touch. Touch me, princess. Give me any justification to take you, to wipe them from your memory, to show how good being touched can feel. I'm no better than them, because I'm seconds from taking you, even if you cried for me to stop. I mean, she *touched* me, unaware how close to snapping my already lax self-control is. She started it.

"I have to know for certain," she whispers.

"Then tell me. Tell me what they have on you."

Just like a rubber band snapping back into place, she retreats, her eyes going back to the frayed edge on the blanket.

Cry, princess.

I want to taste your tears every bit as badly as I want to taste *you*. I shift with her, my hand snatching the back of her neck, pulling her into my orbit more violently than I should've. "Tell me what to do to keep you here." They aren't the words I meant to say, but I'm standing by them.

Her lips part. "I can't leave."

"Princess, I'm asking you what you *need* from me. Say it, and I'll do everything—"

"I kidnapped you." She scoffs, my hand tangling deeper in her messy hair as she tries to struggle free from my hold. It pisses me off more than it should. She's nothing. A score. A rat we're allowing to live in our home. A tool... and everything about her makes me feel bloody and fucking raw.

"I let you kidnap me."

When the neutrality bleeds from her face, I nearly groan. Her eyes are all the more beautiful when she's angry, and I'm not the least bit surprised. "This isn't just about me. This little place you have here? They'll burn it to the ground. If there's even one fucking left, they will not stop until they find me. When they find me, they will take—"

A growl surges from my throat as I slam her back on the mattress. "You think I can't fucking protect you?" My hand tightens, slipping around the front of her delicate neck, my fingers lining up with the yellowed bruising there. Everything in me screams to squeeze, to punish her for even the fucking thought, to cover their marks with ones of my own. "I'd love to see them try. Have you forgotten the gift I gave you? Have you forgotten the way he whimpered and cried out? I did that for *you*."

Her breath is leaving her in pants as I force myself closer to her, her thighs trying to keep me from between her legs. "Stop."

"No."

Her eyes widen, her panting dissolving into ragged breath. "Christian..."

I groan, canting forward to run my nose down the soft slope of her jaw, savoring her sweet, candied scent. "I hated it, you know? Watching that fuck touch you. I hated that fucking look in your eyes, that sad, resolved look. Don't ever look at me like that."

"*You're* the one touching me now!"

"But that's different, isn't it, princess?"

Her hand tangles in my hair, trying to force me away from her, but I'm not going anywhere. "You're just another asshole who thinks they have the fucking right! I'm done! I'm fucking done! Please!" she screams, her anger becoming an entity of its own.

I let her rage against me, letting her fight back, because they never did. When her nails score my skin, her fists beating my back, aggravating the cherished wounds she left on me, I don't stop her. Soon enough, she just screams, the same screams I heard in the woods, the ones that lead me back to her, ones that have festered and built for years. I wouldn't dare stop her from venting them on whatever, or whoever, she wanted. I'd prepare the room, line the walls with bodies, and wipe away the gore until her pain quieted, until she took back the pound of flesh the universe owes her.

"I watched you since your debut. I studied everything you did, obsessed over every little move you made. I knew I would need you, that I would take, you long before I was given the order."

"No! Fuck you! I fucking hate you! I fucking hate you! You should've fucked off, fucking left me there! You have no idea—"

She doesn't stop screaming, but I block it out, my lips teasing her ear, ensuring she hears me. "I don't know when it changed, when you stopped being a tool I wanted to *use* and turned into *someone*. Someone I wanted, *want*." Because, much to my horror, I *do* want the Blood Princess. I want her in my bed, to see what it looks like when she smiles, if she's even capable. I want her lips, her violence, the delicate thing she hides deep in her shell. I want to fix her, fix the damage they did, then break her all over again.

I've never kissed anyone as gently as I do her, and even when her teeth score my lip, I keep kissing her, leaving my blood smeared across her jaw, down her slender neck.

"You had no right!"

"I had every right; you gave it to me, remember?"

Wetness smears across the side of my face—tears. "I didn't, I didn't know! You've jeopardized everything! Oh god—"

"You saw me when I broke that restraint. You knew the moment you led me to that car. You *knew*."

When the first sob wracks her small frame, it resonates in my chest, doing something ugly there. Suddenly, she's not angry—she's just broken. Apprehension settles in my chest. I don't know what she needs. Gentle isn't something that comes naturally to me, so I stay still, so deadly still. She sobs, her fists not pounding my back anymore, but fisting there, clinging to me. She's still too, like she's scared I'll leave, that there will be no one left to witness her tears.

It's at that moment I decide killing the brothers isn't enough. That's the moment I decide to take more.

One Sullivan for every tear she cried, the ones that went unseen.

I can't give her the gentle touch she needs, I can't balm her wounds with soft, patient passes, but violence, vengeance—I can give her that.

"Are they dead?" she hiccups against me.

"Yes, princess. They're dead." I don't know if what I said was a lie. There was no surviving what happened to Anton and Jax, but Vince... I didn't check. Too fucking concerned with her to give a fuck. I cleared the house of anyone, staff and otherwise, a room full of women too drugged out to even notice their impending death, but all of this was sloppy. Unplanned. I'm not known for being reasonable, not accustomed to thinking things through, at all really, but this, even by my standards, was a shit show.

I breathe her in, focusing on the way her heart beats against my chest.

10
Bedmates

Christian

I ignore Jesse as he stalks beside us, the princess curled into my chest as she sleeps, her cheeks raw from tears.

"He's not going to like this," he comments, *loudly*.

"Lower your voice, or I'll punch you in the fucking throat," I growl, fighting the urge to glance down and make sure she's still sleeping—not that I care.

"How do you intend to do that if you're carrying her? *Why* are you carrying her?"

My teeth score my inner lip, the flesh swelling from her bite. "She's staying with me."

"Pardon?" He jogs ahead, blocking my path, his dirty blonde hair tied up in a bun.

"Move, Jesse."

"Explain Christian, because I've got a date tonight, and it doesn't involve having to break up a fight between you and our father."

Of all my eleven siblings, why is it that Jesse was the only one who decided to stay in the compound full time? Right, because the world has a fucked sense of humor. My leg kicks out, my boot connecting roughly with his dick. I don't need to check that my hit landed when he doubles over, gagging.

"That's fucking cheap," he grunts, his forehead pressed to the hardwood floors that always smell like pine.

"I asked you to move," I offer, stepping around him and heading towards my wing.

Jesse is only twenty-two, with a fuck ton of maturing and learning to be done, preferably with hard lessons. With so many siblings and countless mothers, we've always been scattered. Jesse, Dezmond, and Marley stayed with the family business, the latter two deciding to stay off the grounds unless they're needed here for work. All my other relatives I haven't so much as glimpsed in five years. Once we were grown, Father let his ex-wife, the one we all knew as Mom *despite all of us having different mothers*, take over the family house, moving to the compound full time. I went too.

Never left. I'm too good, too engrained in this life to go now.

I was the legacy son, the eldest. I'm the one they come to when they need help. When a deal doesn't go right, when the math isn't adding up, I'm the fixer. Every deal, every heist, every transaction goes through me. The Blood Princess, the Sullivan brothers, they were a problem—my problem. Right now? We can't afford any mistakes, no distractions. I repeat that in my head as I lay *my* mistake in my bed, pulling the dark comforter up around her.

Lana

Trust is a strange thing. It starts as a dent in well-formed armor. The armor you build around yourself to protect all your spongy insides. It's a little dent in an otherwise flawless façade. What damage can a little dent do, after all? The answer is a lot. That little dent marks the way for the axe before it's driven into your heart.

It's been three hours since I woke in Christian's bedroom, snuggled under the covers. Like a bug in a rug, Mom used to say. My face is crusty from the tears I let him see. He took them, absorbed them until I had none left to give. He *held* me. No sex, despite the fact that his hard length was pressed into me the entire time. Daunting, *promising*. His eyes were wild with want as he pinned me to the mattress. I kept waiting for him to jerk down my pants, for his hands to wander. I'm not sure at what point the anxious waiting stopped, and I realized... I wished he would.

Hope is a strange thing.

Christian's bedroom is very much *him*. Severe, hard lined, something serious, but in a crazed way. The tall windows are draped in heavy curtains, a shade or two lighter than the smoky gray walls around it. I haven't seen the rest of the building I'm in, but already, the sleek modern room seems to disagree with the elaborate crown molding. The floor to ceiling bookshelf where each book is turned backwards, hiding the spines, should be a criminal offense. I don't test the handle of the heavy door, knowing in my bones that it's locked and hoping Christian is the only one with a key.

Lana, Five Years Ago

My knocks only barely cut through the pounding music coming from Lewis' room. "Lewis! Open the door!" Exasperated, I turn towards Mom, already knowing I won't get any help. Her face scrunches up, her eyes fixed on her phone in her hands, but I can still see them glistening from over here. I gesture for her to step in, to help, say something, *anything*.

She goes out of her way to not look at me. My chest tightens as I drag in enough air to fill my lungs to capacity, only releasing it on the fourth time my forehead thuds against his bedroom door. "We have to be at the clinic in half an hour! It'll take me forty-five to drive there!"

Please. Please open the door.

It's been a week since Lewis came back home, a week since he's touched drugs. I'd never imagined having him back here would be more nerve-wracking than when he's gone. It's a sword I wake up to hanging over my head, over his too. As hard as I fought to get him home, I hadn't spent a ton of time on the next steps. Sure, I'd researched, read every article, but that was half the problem. The information was there, but now, there's a heaviness to the relief. Somehow, all the right answers don't manage to connect in the real world.

"I'm coming in if you don't open the door!"

My fist is numb from the banging, my head throbbing from the music blaring. It's been constant this week, drowning out the sound of his groans and retching as he struggles through withdraws, but neither of us had the balls to ask him to turn it down.

My footsteps are heavy as I stalk to the kitchen, jerking a butter knife from the drawer. We're both too old for this shit. I'm too old to be living at home, forsaking a true college experience, commuting over an hour and a half to school because Mom can't help but enable him. All he needs to do is show up looking haggard, spitting some shit about being hungry or owing someone money, and she forks over what she has.

Which isn't much anymore.

Online shopping is more exciting than watching your only son deteriorate, engaging in a several years long suicide, more interesting than watching your daughter walk around the house like an anxiety riddled poltergeist. A house that used to be home, one that held so many smiles growing unfamiliar and cold when nothing even changed. The furniture is the same, the well-loved lazy boy with a rip hidden behind a throw blanket that always hangs over the back. The kitchen cabinet has a dent in the wood from Lewis' skateboard years ago. Stickers are still fused to the walls of my light pink bedroom. I put them there in middle school. Nothing about the house is different. It's the lives that filled it that soured. My hand twists the handle, working the butter knife into the mechanism, something I've done so many times by now that it's easy. Far too easy.

When the door gives, the musty air hits me all at once. Dirty socks and cheap body spray. "Shit, would it kill you to crack a window?"

Lewis is lying in bed, his arm draped over his face, shaggy blonde hair matted to the pillow. I only allow myself a few seconds to glare at him before stalking over to his computer. My eyes roll to the back of my head so hard, I damn near hemorrhage as I close out the music, then the still-open porn behind it.

"Lewis, let's go now!"

That strange tightness in my chest returns when he doesn't move. Like every worst-case scenario, I kept myself awake with suddenly became real. "Lewis?"

His skin is palled, clammy, his eyes as far off as I've ever seen them. I jerk his covers off him, my heart dropping at the sight of vomit on his sunset orange sheets. "Hey!" My hands are frantic as I shake him, tears filling my eyes. "Mom!"

He's always been so much bigger than me, even now. He's heavy as I jerk him up into my arms, not giving a damn about the vomit I'm being smeared with. "Mom, help me!"

Every video I've ever watched to prepare me for this moment evades me, my own vomit creeping up my throat as my little brother makes a sound more fitting to a zombie than a human. "Mom, please! Get my bag! Get the Narcan now!" I pinch his cheek roughly, so hard that I'm sure it'll bruise. He gurgles, milky foam leaking from the corner of colorless lips.

Please, please.

Mom is frantic when she finally enters the room, all but throwing my bag at me as she dissolves into sobs. I barely recognize her as the strong, independent woman who worked two jobs since the time I was two.

Lewis drops from my arms as I empty out the contents, my hands trembling as they find the nasal applicator. "Call 911!" I scream at her as her crying grows louder, tilting his head back before pushing down on the plunger.

"Please, please, please, please," I mumble as I wait, rubbing at his chest, my heart thudding painfully in mine like it's trying to work for the both of us. When he comes around, it's all at once. He lurches up so quickly, he headbutts me, retching.

"Yes, he's up now!" Mom's voice filters in as I rub my brother's back and arms, trying to get his attention.

"You're okay, you're okay."

I don't know if I'm telling him or myself as his warm colored eyes turn on me, finally registering his surroundings. "What the fuck?" he mumbles, looking more irritated than anything.

"You overdosed, Lewis! I just had to give you fucking Narcan." My voice is shrill even to my own ears, but holy shit, I can't breathe.

When he tries to stand up, I scramble. "No, you need to sit down until—"

His hands brace on my chest, keeping me back. "No, Lana, I don't need to do shit. It's your fucking fault this dumb shit even happened!"

"Lewis, knock it off. This is serious!" Mom yells, still sobbing.

Lewis shoves me, hard. I'd never realized before how gentle he'd been, how much he held back each time I tried to stop him from leaving. My back collides with the metal display shelf, knocking the breath from my lungs. Our eyes only meet for a moment, and for a moment, I think he might stop. He might say sorry, but he doesn't.

Then, he's gone.

This time, I don't run after him.

By the time daylight streams through the heavy curtains, Christian hasn't returned. As it turns out, after years of constant company, silence is deafening. It feels less like the gift I thought it would be and more like something being inflicted upon me—a slight, a punishment for a crime I can't identify. My head is light from my back-and-forth pacing. Christian's books are all pulled from their shelves, some replaced with the spine facing out. Most of them are still littering the ground. I had intended to just fill the space my nightmarish thoughts were taking up but messing up his room felt... *good*. For once, I didn't think I would get hurt for doing something I wasn't supposed to. I had no reasonable explanation for feeling that way, only that none of the brothers had ever held me like that, not even Vince. Being consumed by him might be something I could get used to.

When the key turns in the door, my heart lurches into my throat, threatening to suffocate me. My feet edge towards the bed, muscle memory demanding I go there, knowing that's where I'll end up, but

I don't. Relief hits me like a whip as Christian's wavy, dark hair comes into focus. Imagine that: feeling relief at the sight of someone holding you against your will. I remember reading a true crime book years ago about some creepy fuck and his wife who took a young girl. In the end, she defended them at the trial meant to vindicate her. Stockholm syndrome, they called it. I didn't understand it then, couldn't imagine *wanting* your abuser, until Christian. His veins strain against bronzed skin and his lips couldn't be soft, yet I know they are.

He looks exhausted. Dark circles only seem to enhance the effectiveness of his brooding green eyes. His dress shirt is rumpled, but the stain on the collar catches my attention. *Blood*. When his eyes command mine, it seems to exhaust him further.

"I see you've made yourself acquainted with my bookshelf."

"The spines were backwards."

"It's my bedroom."

"It's a crime against books."

His eyebrows rise at that. In the matter of a step, he's gone from trudging into a room to stalking. My eyes find the blood on his collar as he undoes his shirt, willing myself to not look at his chest.

I fail.

"Perhaps you preferred the room downstairs, princess."

"Perhaps I preferred the place you took me from." It's a lie, one that feels like ash on my tongue.

He cocks his head at that, almost too much, and he leaves it that way as he rounds me, stalks me. "Is that so? Missing home then?" His voice is velvet but hidden in the folds of fabric is a razor blade, one determined to *cut*.

I take a step back, anticipating the comfortable dread to pool in my stomach, something to snuff out the heat. It never comes. My core clenches around nothing, my thighs pressing together as my back hits the now mostly empty bookshelf. My body's sense of betrayal doesn't surprise me. I learned too early on to take pleasure when it's offered, but somehow, this situation feels deceptively different.

His green eyes are no longer tired, the only evidence of the worn man from seconds ago lingering in the bags under his eyes. "Perhaps we should make a trip back, see if their cocks have decomposed yet. Perhaps they've even bloated a bit." The smell of liquor hits me as he comes close enough to tower over me. "Might feel good, being filled to capacity for once." The words leave him in a growl, my heart beating so violently in my chest, it feels like it will never calm. His words flame the anger that has been building in my soul for years now, long before I bartered myself to the Sullivan brothers.

I don't recall making the decision to hurt him, only that the moment my hand rises to strike, he catches it halfway to his face. "Fuck. You." The words leave my lips like an omen, a curse.

"Yes, I'd quite like that."

The next moment is crushing lips and teeth, a passion I've had inflicted on me more times than I can count, but this time? *I'm* inflicting. It's a kiss meant to consume, to erase all others. One that for the first time, I give willingly.

11
Fist

<u>Fully Alive by Flyleaf</u>

After twelve hours spent tracking down the remains of the Sullivan brothers, I had looked forward to sleep. The last thing I'd expected upon my arrival home was to be kissing the Blood Princess. Kissing doesn't seem quite enough to describe the way she savagely takes my mouth. My cock and heart ratchet to attention, every pulse in my body screaming to double the violence, the intensity. Blood whooshes in my ears as she gives herself over, her small body melting into mine.

The need to dominate forces a sinew deep throb to my cock, but I match her instead. I let her push and pull, nip and wither.

I let the princess tell me what she needs. Again, in the same 24 hours, I find myself the sponge, absorbing the cast offs of her pain, her violence. I take it all willingly, greedily, a starving beggar in the streets. She's a tool, not a fucking lifeline. Yet, from the moment she led me to that SUV, I've clung to her like one.

"Take me," she gasps against my lips.

All I can muster is a groan, hitching her trembling legs around my hips, grinding into her as she wraps around me, fusing to my frame like she's always been there. This tiny, broken thing decimates me with a roll of her hips. When her back meets the bookshelf with a slam, my hand snaps out, steadying the thing, bracing against it.

"Do it," she taunts, goading me, her tongue urging mine in needy little swirls. When my hand grips her rounded ass, squeezing it, the slight wince I feel pulls everything into blinding, cursed clarity.

I try to ignore it; fuck, I really do.

"Princess…" I warn, because I don't fucking care.

I don't.

I really shouldn't.

Her cunt grinds against me, offering every piece of bliss I've ached for since the moment I saw her, and I pull back. My cock weeps for the loss of pressure as I carry her to the bed. Each pass of her nails on my back does far more than my princess bargained for—it marks me, claims me for her. She claws, nips, and goads me into exactly what I what.

What I need.

To obliterate her.

She gasps as I lay her back on the bed, my hand clasping around her hip. Fuck, she's gorgeous, with her knotted red hair, wide golden eyes looking up at me like I just wrote the lines of her favorite book. "Easy, princess. You'll tear your stitches."

"I don't care," she breathes, a needy little sound that damn near drives me to the brink. "Hurt me."

The newly unfamiliar organ in my chest makes another odd flip. "I won't; not until you're ready."

Fucking hell, that sounds dumb, even to me.

Her eyes widen, her brows quirking up before knitting together. The gray sweatshirt she's wearing rode up, exposing her stomach. I want to explore every grove and dip of her flesh, but fuck me, I can't look away from her eyes.

Her sad fucking eyes.

"Don't fucking lie to me," she whispers, suddenly so still.

The words are on the tip of my tongue, a promise I can't keep, because she's here for a reason, and it's not to keep my dick wet, heart racing, or my bed warm.

"I won't take your cunt until you're ready."

It's all I can give her, and fuck, the look in her eyes, the sudden admiration like I'm some knight who just swooped her off her feet. I'm not a good guy, not by any stretch of the imagination, but I'm self-aware enough to know if that good guy showed up, sword in hand, to take her away, I'd blow an RPG-sized hole in his chest and fist fuck the cavity. I'm the cruelty my princess has pretended to be, the monster they made her.

The monster I refuse to let her kill.

Lana

For a moment, I think he'll leave, that the thudding in my heart will scare him away. When he pulls back, my hands fly out on their own accord, knotting in his hair. Those harsh lips pull up in a smirk. "I'm not going anywhere."

Again, his words tunnel past my ribcage, settling deep in my chest like a blade, one I'm scared I'll never be able to dislodge. That's the funny thing about trust and the horrid thing about hope. Once it sparks in an unrelenting darkness, it's damn near impossible to snuff out.

His head dips as he lowers himself, inhaling deeply at the crux of my thighs. "Fuck, princess. I bet you're soaking wet for me."

I don't even try to suppress the moan that comes unbidden to my lips. I'm fully clothed but bare. He's a live wire, and I'm the suicidal manic jonesing for a touch. Something, anything, that's fully mine, untouched by hands that didn't belong.

I'm all need. A greedy fucking little girl who wants to be touched—badly.

But I don't want the hero with stunning blonde hair and piercing blue eyes. I want the villain. I want his pain, his violence, because I know he can stomach mine.

For the first time in forever, I don't want to be saved.

The moment that passes is harsh. It's raw, and together, we manage to come to a conclusion, one that I'm sure equally ensures our destruction. Christian crawls back up to me, his lips stealing mine again before they fuse to my chin, tracking the line of my jaw to my neck. It's not kisses he leaves in his wake; its tongue and teeth. He wrenches up my sweatshirt, rubbing the gray fabric against my oversensitive skin, exposing my breasts. "Fucking hell."

I feel my cheeks flush as he nibbles his way down the valley of my breasts, a shudder rolling down my spine as he laps at one of my puckered nipples, eliciting a very needy sound. His green eyes are on me when I wrench mine open, desperately bowing my back off the bed, as if it'll force him to take my nipple into his mouth. He blows gently, the cool air only adding to the dampness between my legs.

"Christian," I moan, arching into him further, desperate to rub against him despite his bruising hold on my hip. "Please."

He groans, switching sides to torment my other nipple. "Such a pretty word. Say it again."

I'd like to say I held out, that I teased him too, but I folded like a deck of cards, need blinding me.

"Please, please, please, make me feel good."

He rolls his hips into me as his teeth capture my nipple, biting and tugging gently. I'm all sensation, my heart and clit pounding in tune.

He keeps my nipple caged between his teeth as his tongue flicks and teases, his teeth adding pressure, slowly but surely, until pain mixes with the pleasure.

When his hand leaves my hip, his body lifting off me enough to find purchase on my swollen clit, I moan loudly, trying to grind into him.

"Pretty princess, you look even better like this than I'd imagined you would." His words are mumbled from my nipple, gravelly.

He takes a mile and allows me an inch, the pressure on my nipple mounting as he makes too-soft circles on my clit with long, deft fingers. Through the thick sweatpants, it's maddening. I mewl and plead as he torments me, my breath hitching when the pressure of his teeth on my nipple is too much, too painful, forcing my impending orgasm back just as it surges to the surface.

Then, he lets go.

Pain and sensation rip back into my redden, swollen nipple just as he jerks down my pants.

His mouth lands on my clit, feasting on it. My scream breaks off halfway as I explode, his tongue lapping at my cunt as I grind into him, riding out wave after wave of pleasure. Once my hips slow, my back collapsing from its arched position, he blows again, cool air assaulting my throbbing core. A bone deep shudder leaves me as my skin breaks out in goosebumps, my legs trembling as I loosen my death grip on the sheets.

"Fuck," he curses. My head snaps down, expecting to find him angry as he lifts backing away. It couldn't have been more wrong.

Strong, calculated, wild, and severe, Christian looks flustered, reverent. He drags his hand through his knotted hair, and I can see his self-control teeter, balancing on a blade.

Hurt me.

I can take it.

My heart drops as he roughly jerks his phone out of his pocket, holding it up in front of him. "What are you doing?"

The words are breathy; I want to close my legs to hide myself, but I stay still as he ignores me. The sound of a camera shudder wipes out my post-orgasm haze. "Why?"

"New phone. I've been meaning to change my wallpaper."

My mouth pops open as I lift myself from the bed, the action pulling at my stitches. "You can't!"

"Why not?" He taps on the phone a few more times before he holds it out for me to see.

I feel my cheeks darken further. I look... like someone else. He holds the phone steady as I readjust my clothes, crawling forward to get a better look. My red hair is fanned out and wild behind me, my eyes heavy with lust. There's color in my pale cheeks—real color, not the kind that someone painted on. Even my many bruises look prettier than they do when I look at them in the mirror. None of that is what makes an uncomfortable sensation settle in my gut. It's the look in my eyes, a dangerous look.

It's different seeing your own stupidity reflected back at you.

When I pull away, he locks his phone, pocketing it as if I might try to snatch it away. The thought of having my breasts and cunt on his phone is adding to that dangerous feeling, like this is more than it is, like it's a mutual obsession.

"You should change that," I whisper.

He groans as he adjusts his thick cock tented in his pants. "Not a chance."

I smile.

Stupid Lana.

12
Heart

Christian

"The blood princess has resumed eating," my father comments, staring intently at a handful of files as he shovels toast into his mouth.

My hand twitches to reach out and flip my phone face down. With my luck, the screen will wake up and show her to him. Turns out, setting her exposed body, as beautiful as it is, as my lock screen isn't good for productivity.

I force neutrality to my face, despite the slur of red blaring lights and sirens sounding in my head.

"Perhaps next time, you won't have such intense feelings about my methods." I don't mention those methods include taking time out of my day to feed her dinner, that I pop in at lunch when I can, that I reward her with mind shattering orgasms when I get word she finished her meals. I definitely don't fucking mention that I wait until she falls asleep at night and gently scoot her over until she's nestled against me.

He makes a noncommittal sound, taking a deep swallow of scalding coffee, his deeply scarred fingers on display. "Then she should be ready to return to work as soon as Dr. Lamaison gives her the all clear. We've readied her announcement stream; a coronation, Jesse called it. Quite clever."

I open my mouth, some shitty excuse he won't buy already formed on my tongue when he speaks first.

"You will find other hobbies to fill your time when she returns to work, yes?"

"My job will be done," I respond carefully, because the idea of sending her back down into that bare basement room makes me want to see if I could fit his entire coffee mug down his throat.

I could. With a little work.

My phone buzzes, and I adjust, moving my newspaper over the screen, hiding the picture of Lana sleeping in my bed. She's lying on her stomach, her face almost hidden beneath a curtain of red hair. I had to change it from the centerfold version after I killed a member of my security team for accidentally glimpsing it on my phone. I took the new picture a week ago, and hundreds since. It's been a week and a half since I brought her back up to my room, since I realized I was falling, rapidly. Hurtling from fifty thousand feet, by the time I recognized my impending doom, I was already halfway down. With each day, it's become glaringly obvious that I will hurt her.

Irreparably, even.

So today, when I stalked towards my office, I forced myself to continue. I could hear the disappointment in her voice as she thanked the girl who delivered her lunch tray, saw her smile die as I passed. She'd *smiled*. I wanted to capture her screams, her fear, violence, anger. I spent years anticipating the way she'd shrivel as I forced her to perform for us. Instead, I made her smile.

That smile was the end of us both.

Me and Lana Marie Porter.

When I lift my eyes from the papers in front of me, I meet my father's.

Hard and unyielding.

Seeing far too much, just like he always has.

Christian, Nine Years Old

The sound of snarling and screams jolts me from where I'd dozed off on the couch. When my eyes pop open, blurry from sleep, they focus on the color red pooling quickly in our pristine white living room.

Zeke, my German Shepard, is standing over my little sister, her blue eyes wide with fear as he snarls.

Hadley flinches, and that's all it takes for his teeth to meet her shoulder, jerking and growling. Panic slams up my gut as I bolt from the couch, my throat tightening with fear as Hadley screams for Father, her tiny voice echoing off the walls.

My hands throb and ache as I yell, smack, and heave, desperately trying to dislodge my dog from her. It's then that Zeke lets go long enough to let her body slump and for him to bear down harder on my little sister's neck and shake, the force of his attack pushing her into the plush carpet.

"Hadley!"

The silence that follows is deafening and Hadley's small hands, with her yellow chipped nail polish, are so still where they're knotted in his fur, her neck bent at an angle between his jaws.

The silence only lasts seconds, but it feels like a lifetime before mom starts screaming. Father rushes in front of me, disrupting the scene of white splattered with red. His calm demeanor edged by his own fear as he bends, wrenching his hands into Zeke's mouth, fighting his jaws open seconds before his boot connects roughly with my dog's neck.

BATHED IN BLOOD

Zeke yelps loudly, still snarling frantically, trying to maul his way out from underneath my father's boot. More panic now than aggression.

It's not until Mom gathers up Hadley, rushing her outside, away from the bloody scene, that my brain catches up. I realize I was screaming too, that I hadn't stopped. Vomit surges up my throat, my hand flying up to stop it from spewing. The slick warmth of my hands smearing on my lips in the process, the rough texture of fur scratching at my skin. When Fathers' eyes meet mine, he doesn't have to give a voice to the look on his face.

This is your fault.

I'm frantically wiping the blood off my face, my body trembling. He'd nagged me for months to train Zeke, to keep him out of the family room where my sister played. He was my dog, my first dog, my responsibility. It was my job to correct him when he'd started nipping her. He'd only done it once; she'd pulled his fur. I...

I vomit on the carpet, heaving violently, and when I look back up, Father's gone and so is Zeke, my head light on my shoulders as I follow the trail of blood outside.

Follow the sounds of the screams.

And later that night, when they come back from the hospital, their clothes remain smeared with blood, and they don't have Hadley with them. Mom doesn't even look at me as she passes, a hollow agony in her bright blue eyes.

My tears are hot on my face, my throat burning from my sobs and apologies as Father leads me out to the backyard, forcing his gun into hands that never stopped shaking. As I approach, my dog's mouth is still crusted with Hadley's blood, and his tail wags excitedly. Father's deep voice is thick with emotion.

His dark eyes are bloodshot and puffy. "Never let anything come between you and your family again, son."

I won't.
I swear.

13
Backing

*L*ana

When dinner rolls around, I find myself pacing again. My bottom lip is raw from where I've chewed it. He skipped lunch, which is fine. Entirely fine. Understandable, even. He's a busy man, a busy man who I've shared a bed with for the past week and a half. The very man who's fed me for nearly every meal. Listened attentively as he leaned against the opposite wall, cock engorged and arms crossed while I enjoyed a long shower, blabbering on for so long that my throat hurt, explaining different weather systems, some of the most catastrophic storms to ever hit land and why they happened, like I was trying to fit four years of silence into an hour.

In order for a tornado, tsunami, or hurricane to form, all the right ingredients have to be in place at the right time. Pressure systems, temperature... it all has to come together to make a worst-case scenario.

That's what this is: a worst-case scenario, all coming together in the perfect way. Somewhere within these two weeks, he got the ingredients right. Maybe it's because he didn't fuck me, even when I begged. Maybe it's the way he'd hum to himself, long after he thought I'd fallen asleep. I'd lay still, keeping my breath even as his hands combed through my hair. He'd whisper stories, some so outlandish that if I hadn't seen what he was capable of firsthand, I'd think he was lying. Everything that feels right is so wrong that I've started fucking talking.

I can taste the food he brings.

I haven't tasted food in years.

And most horrifying?

I look forward to him every night, his warmth when he stalks in, dark and watchful. Hanging on to his self-control by a hairpin, he undresses, showers, and tugs me into bed with him. If I've eaten well, taken my medication that they no longer sneak into my food, and do all the basic self-care things that seemed too taxing at the beginning, he makes me come apart on his tongue, fingers, thighs, but never cock.

He's denied me every time I've begged to return the favor, my mouth salivating at the thought of him.

Despite his father's threats, I haven't performed.

A dangerous, smoldering seed of hope has infiltrated my chest. Even if I spend the rest of my life between these four gray walls, it would be worth it to avoid being *her*.

I drag my nails across my thigh, scratching a phantom itch where they branded me, the skin raised and angry. I can feel her even now, my nails chewed down to the quick, and I'd be lying if I said I hadn't been... craving the release a performance offers, an outlet for all the anxiety and rage. Someone's screams that aren't my own, someone's pain I don't feel.

But Christian hasn't hurt me, not in any way I didn't want him to.

The perfect storm.

Catastrophic when it makes landfall.

A category five, without a doubt.

My eyes linger on the circle branded into my thigh: the Sullivan S in old English font, J, A, and V woven into the ornate border. They had it custom made for me. I've been careful, so careful, to keep it hidden, as if him seeing it would prove what I really am: an animal that needed to be cowled. Tamed. Forced again into servitude.

With it on display, I'm an exposed wire that just spasmed in a nearby puddle. My breasts are full, my nipples already peaked, my core wet and throbbing with anticipation. Christian has respected me. He kept his promise. I wasn't ready; I hadn't healed. He doesn't know that what I've been made into is a being *past* healing. My physical wounds are nearly gone, bruises faded back into my pale skin. The other ones, deeper ones, will never stop festering. I turn in the mirror, studying myself from another angle, my long red hair dripping in waves down my back, stopping just underneath my shoulder blades.

I want Christian Vanegas to be the one to rewrite the past four years of my life. I chose him.

I get to fucking choose.

Another hour passes, another sixteen trips to the bathroom to check my subtle makeup, to reapply the perfume he brought me. Another two or three times, I carefully removed his expensive bottle of aftershave, inhaling the deep sandalwood and bergamot.

When the lock turns, I can't stop the gasp that leaves my mouth. Suddenly, my nudity feels like a terrible choice—too forward, *desperate*. I haven't had to try to seduce a man... ever. I'm inexperienced in consent, and it's all occurring to me right now. The door swings open harder than usual, Christian's dark green eyes glaring holes in the floor as he stalks in.

My legs move without my permission, taking a step back, even though all I want is to fly forward, pressing every inch of my body against his. Lana would beg him; the princess would demand.

I want to demand it tonight, to take because he lets me.

I want it all.

"Hi," I breathe. *Fucking hi? Fucking hi, Lana?*

His eyes jerk up from the hardwood, and the cold look he gives me sinks straight into my bones. If it had lasted longer than a few seconds, I might've dissolved into tears on the spot, but then, he *sees* me. Christian's eyes dip to my breasts, now heaving violently in tune with the unforgiving way my lungs are forcing air in and out. When his eyes dip lower, towards my throbbing core, I shift, opening my legs enough to let him see how wet I already am, how badly I want this.

Need it.

I need to take this back.

My choice. I need it to be him.

My savior, protector, kidnapper, and tormentor.

"Fucking hell," he breathes out, tossing a black tote bag to the floor beside him before burying both hands in his hair. His angry tone has me taking another step back, my entire being begging me to lay down.

To be small.

I don't.

"I'm healed. Dr. Lamaison said—"

"Don't say another man's name while you're fucking looking at me like that."

My tongue dips out, wetting my raw bottom lip, the sting a welcome distraction from the horrid smile that threatens to overtake my face. The door slams loudly as he kicks it shut behind him.

"I'm ready, Christian. I want you."

His thick brows knit together as he drags his large hands down his face, shaking his head.

My stomach wiggles its way free from my throat, dropping down past my knees. My hands drag up to shield my breasts, my thighs squeezing tightly, like there's any damn point in hiding myself now. I can already taste the acid like rejection on my tongue. It's only mollified by the obvious heat in his eyes, the swell of his cock pressing against his pants.

How can someone's gaze feel every bit as exhilarating as a touch?

When his heated perusal stops, it's not hard to guess why. His hands drop from his face like boulders, his wavy hair shifting into his eyes as he cocks his head, those damming eyes latching onto the brand on my upper hip.

His jaw clenches as he stares, like he's waiting for it to change, like his eyes are betraying him. My hand shoots down before I can stop it, covering the brand. It was the wrong move.

When those eyes turn back on me, I remember why I thought Christian was a thunderstorm. The violent, unforgiving way he looks at me sends my heart bracketing in my chest. When he bends, scooping the tote off the ground, I actually flinch.

I'm defenseless as I stare at the bundle he pulls out, stalking across the wide room with barely suppressed rage, shoving it into my waiting hands. "Get dressed, Lana."

Lana?

Tears spring to my eyes, my head snapping up to meet his, away from the deep green lingerie. My hair tickles my back as I take another step, this one forcing me to sit on the bed. "Don't. Please."

Christian's eyes are dead, empty, from the ones I've grown accustomed to the past two weeks as he reaches in the bag again. "We're on a time limit. You're on in forty."

Vomit surges in my gut as he pulls out my mask, tossing it beside me on the bed, emotion clogging my throat as I open my mouth, only to promptly close it.

14
Implosion

Christian

I'm a fucking bastard.

I ignore Jesse's stare as I pace the studio, my own reflection mocking me in the wide screens that line the front wall. See, the thing that always set us apart from others in the industry was that we offer a more...*interactive* experience. The viewer chooses the angle, the zoom, the pace. It gives the sick fucks willing to dish out thousands for a seat on our docket the illusion of control. We film the violence in 4k, 360-degree views, catering to virtual reality if you're willing to dish out the funds.

She changed everything. Suddenly, our life's work was second best. The only viewers left in our servers were loyalists who have stuck around when these videos were just my grandfather sending a message to a rival weapons dealer. That's how it all started: first, his eighteen-year-old daughter, his wife, and then, his twin sons. Just a simple hammer and some nails. A classic.

This was long before the time of the dark web, secure servers, VPNs, and shock sites. It was a crudely filmed VHS, state-of-the art for its time. The man sent it around every circle he was in, knowing that eventually, a copy would end up in the correct hands.

He hadn't expected to find an entire community of sick fucks who were willing to pay for more.

There, *Vengeance Vanegas* was born. My eyes fall to the intertwined Vs painted on the wall. For the first time, my pride in what I've grown this into pales. There's a sick feeling in my gut I'm not accustomed to. Vengeance Vanegas was my calling from the very first life I took: my own dog. I'd vomited, sobbed until I vomited again, and then something snapped. I decided he wasn't enough. Somehow, in my adolescent brain, it made sense. I'd lost two people I loved. It was my fault; the pain made it impossible to breathe. The weight on my chest was unlike anything I'd ever experienced before. At the time, the only way to ease the weight was to share it. Take two more lives, even the odds. When my father found our gardener and then one of the night watchmen the next morning, we both knew there was no going back. No unturning the page. No *fixing* me.

Vengeance Vanegas became my calling. My purpose. It was how I could serve my family after all I'd done to harm it.

My penance.

It was just a bonus that I enjoyed the line of work. I'd have done it either way. That has never been more evident than in this moment, the crowning moment of my career. *Our* princess. *My* princess.

I should be tossing back shots, giddy and rock hard, awaiting her first performance. Already, our sales have toppled their previous high. Luca, our tech guy, is nearly soaked through with sweat just trying to keep the servers up. It's a historical moment in the snuff industry. A stolen princess. A kidnapped icon in her own right.

The confirmation of a deity.

I should be proud, but all I can see is that sad fucking look in her eyes. I'd wanted to talk to her, rambled on in my head for hours about how I would explain, how I would try to make her understand why I couldn't fail at this, at least until I found a way out. She had to be the Blood Princess. I wanted to tell her, Lana, that I... God, that I fucking can't breathe until I slip back into that bedroom with her. My bedroom that no longer smells like me, one where I find silky strands of red hair on fucking everything.

Where she reorganized my bookshelf. By color.

A fucking rainbow. It's the most hideous thing I've ever seen but I wouldn't dare change it.

How even in her vulnerable, quiet moments, when she's lost and sad, she hurls sunlight into a space that has never seen it before. I want to hear more about the clouds. It's all on the tip of my tongue.

If I could single-handedly capture a snuff icon, bring down our only real competitor, bust my ass for the past three weeks organizing the end of the Sullivan family line...*I could tell a woman I had fucking fallen so damn hard for her, it feels like my brain will explode.*

Then, I saw the brand. How had I fucking missed it?

Their fucking symbol on *my* princess.

It wasn't her fault. God, it wasn't her fault.

But I wanted to hurt her for it.

I did, in the worst way possible because again, I'm a fucking bastard.

Neither of us remembers how to communicate in terms of love and kindness, but she and I undoubtedly speak the same violent language. It was force fed to us until we gorged. She'll understand. She'll have to, even if she hates the way it tastes. She'll have me, even if the violence chokes her to fucking death.

The sound of heels clicking on polished floors halts me in my tracks, my head snapping towards the door. When Jesse snickers, I level my glare at him, hoping it would burn a hole in his throat. It doesn't. When the heels stop, I'm having a hard time turning my eyes back to the owner. It's the widening, appreciative look in my brother's eyes that forces me to face her.

My knuckles pop.

The guard behind her simply nods, mentioning a few things I can't focus on. I wrack my brain, trying to identify every member of staff who would've seen her on her path down here. She glares at me, and I meet it tenfold, my voice strained. "I left a robe for you."

She drags a deep breath through her lungs, making her pert nipples push even harder against the satin fabric of the lingerie I chose for her. It's more befitting a nun than the Blood Princess. The silk top cuts low into her cleavage, the back doing the same in a deep V, the top ending just above her delicate bellybutton, one I've tasted more times than I can count in the past two weeks. The shorts come up high on the sides, hugging her perfect ass and rounding hips. The deep, emerald green fabric clings to her skin as if it were painted on. I know her ass is bared. My jaw clenches as she turns towards my brother.

Away from me.

My eyes find the place I know their brand sits high on her hip, underneath the clothes. My heart thuds loudly in my chest as that anger from earlier needles away at any valiant good guy intentions I might've deluded myself into having. I told myself I dressed her this way for her, that I did it for her comfort. The princess is *mine*.

The days of having her ass, cunt and tits bared during streams are over. The days of pretending like she isn't mine are over.

"I'd like to begin," she comments casually, pushing her long hair over her shoulders before slipping her mask on.

Jesse's eyes flick to mine. Whatever he sees there makes him shift on his feet. "Yeah, that's more of Christian's domain. I'm just here for the show."

My sweet, sad Lana is nowhere to be seen as my princess glimpses at me over her shoulder. I can feel her amber eyes through the eerie doll mask before she turns away. It's like being held captive in the desert before being dropped ass first into Siberia. Weeks of having her gentle hands and soft kisses make this version of her seem more severe. This is the woman from my dreams, the one I watched for hours, the one who teased me, giggling and twirling like a child while I laid on her table.

She laughs, not a real one. No, it's a focused, flirty sounding thing, and I'm nearly positive I've ruptured a blood vessel in my eye. I'm almost certainly on the fast track to a fucking aneurysm, because so help me Lana, if you speak to him like that again—

"I'll make it a good one then. The guard told me we started in ten, and that was six minutes ago. I'd hate to be late to my own show."

Jesse looks at me, near panicked now. I'm choosing to ignore his chubbed cock, because if I acknowledge it now, I will almost certainly kill a second sibling.

I'm already halfway across the room when my shit-head brother's panicked expression is traded for a smirk. My gun feels feather light as I jerk it from my jacket holster, the ear rattling shot rings out, making my princess flinch, just barely. The guard who escorted her body slumps to the floor as I press the side against her neck, caressing her with it.

"You look stunning, but let's remember whose fingers you've been fucking yourself on for the past two weeks. Speak to him like that again, and running behind schedule will be the last of your concerns."

Her fists tighten at her sides, the mask shifting as she clenches her jaw. "Fingers, tongue, thighs, but what I wanted was a coc—"

My breath leaves me in rough pants as I press the muzzle underneath her chin, forcing her to step back into me, her ass rubbing against my constant erection despite the deafening rage. "Jesse, a moment," I growl against her ear.

My brother's smirk is fully back in place as he dips his head. "It's a pleasure to officially meet you, Blood Princess. You'll fit in just fine here."

I track him as he steps over the guard's body, letting the heavy automatic doors to the lower compound slide shut, pushing the man's body as they do. "Lana—"

She cuts me off, jerking to face me. My hand tightens on the handle of my gun as I quickly move it away, flicking the safety on. "Don't fucking call me that."

My hand itches with the need to touch her as I holster my gun. Since I've decided to no longer deny myself, my hand snaps out, jerking her mask up enough to show her pretty, full lips, my other one capturing the back of her neck. "Never pegged you as a brat."

"Never pegged you as a bitch," she offers. Oh, if sad Lana was gorgeous, pissed off Lana is enough to make me come in my pants like a fucking teenager. She flinches as I run my fingers across her lips, gently. It only barely dampens my erection to know she expected me to hurt her. Doesn't surprise me boys like the Sullivan brothers couldn't handle a little name calling.

"Lana, we need to speak after the stream." She opens her mouth to cut me off, but I insert my thumb instead, making her gag as I push it to the back of her throat. "You don't have to like it, but you'll listen. I am not *them*; my family is not *them*. This doesn't have to hurt."

She bites down, hard, and I only barely bite back a groan as I very painfully extract my fingers from her teeth, leaving a line of spit still connecting us. "It already does."

Her words hit me like a tire iron straight to the skull.

"Sir, two minutes before we're live." The sound comes over the speaker in the viewing room. With that, the wide doors pop open, letting in the screams that were previously contained behind the door.

"What's my theme?" she whispers, pulling away, fixing her mask before facing the door.

I can't help myself as I drag my hand through her hair, the fingers teasing the shin of her back, making her shudder. "Dealer's choice for your first stream back."

She heads into the room, and it takes everything I have to let the doors close behind her. My eyes snap to the large screens as her beautiful, delicate frame fills them. Lana stands still, barely breathing as she awaits her cue. The audio to the room clicks on just as it's given, and she dips into the deep curtsy, flashing a cute little wave to the main camera.

My cock throbs, and my fucking chest hurts as I slump into a chair. My hand is on the master controls, just in case anything goes wrong.

I'm a bastard.

15
Scream

Coming Undone By Korn

Christian

I block out everything but Lana as she makes a show of picking out the tools she intends for the man strapped to the wall. I even almost smile as she pretends to get frustrated by his begging. Her heeled foot stomps against the ground, her red waves flicking over her shoulder as she shushes him. Long, slender fingers tap at the chin of her mask. Immediately, I regret not providing her with gloves. The idea of any part of her actually touching another man makes my leg bob with the effort to stay seated.

"God, oh fucking God! Please just listen, listen to me!" the man pleads, not really saying anything of substance. His entire body trembles as a prominent wet stain grows on the crouch of his boxers, boxers that stayed on because no way in hell am I letting his cock out near her, even if it is just for her to mutilate it.

Lana turns, brandishing the tool of her choice to the camera.

A Heretic's Fork.

Her fingers slide over the leather collar attached to the bi-pronged ends, forming needle sharp points, and she skips over to the man as he thrashes wildly. My hands clench against the armrests as he lashes out, spitting on her mask.

"Fucking bitch! Get the fuck back, you fucking crazy bitch!"

The princess' hands are steady as she wrenches his head forward, tsking at his rabid attempts to bite her. She's safe, entirely in my domain. Fully fitted in metal restraints, the man was screened for any disease, an instant suppression system should something go wrong. Mostly, I'm here, behind doors I can open if she should require me. It doesn't stop me from vibrating with rage every time the cuck's teeth snap towards her exposed arms as she fastens the collar around his thick neck. He fights valiantly as she wrenches his head back up, ensuring the upper forked prongs are situated tightly underneath his chin, the opposite pressing into his chest. If he slips, moves just a little too much, it'll-

The man cries out in pain as he tries to look down, sending the upper and lower prongs into his flesh, not enough to kill him but enough to fucking hurt. My heart thunders as she fiddles with the torso strap, one we've never bothered with before, but I wasn't taking risks today, not with her.

My hand slams on the intercom without my permission. "Do not unstrap—"

She does. His body sags a little lower, that strap having supported a lot of his weight. Fucking hell.

He screams, the prongs again digging into him on either side, a garbled mess of words spilling from his mouth as blood coats his chest, unable to open his mouth to fully cry, beg, or bite.

Luca's eyes meet mine in an irritated glance through the viewing windows into the tech room beside this one. He throws his hands up before refocusing on the screens in front of him. The viewers don't like interference, but I couldn't give less of a fuck.

I'm pacing now as Lana repeats the process, letting him drop further as she releases his upper thigh restraints. The man bellows, the prods now permanently embedded in the tender underside if his jaw.

His eyes roll back in his head. Absently, I recognize an entry request to the room popping up on the hub, approaching it without even glancing who was requesting it on the security feed. My knuckles pop from the force of my clenched fists as I stare at Lana, her chest heaving in short spasms, her hands shaking. I can hear her rapid breaths through the mic.

"Sir, there's been a perimeter breach I wanted to make you aware of," Kallen states at my back.

My princess stalks over to the table, jerking off the first thing she finds: a blow torch. The device roars to life as she aims it at his stomach, being sure to get it close enough to make the skin bubble but not render him useless too soon.

"Sir."

"What?" I snap, spinning on him.

His eyes widen slightly, lowering his head before speaking. "It appears a homeless man wandered onto the back lawn. He was very intoxicated, looked like he'd been out in the woods for a few days. Your father is out, so I—"

"I don't care. Let him go."

"Sir?"

But I've already turned back, barely registering the man anymore as Lana giggles. It's not the cute, endearing one she usually sets loose during her streams. No, it's wild, breathy. She's not okay, and the idea of her being locked in there is suddenly too hard to swallow.

When I take a step forward towards the doors, the sound of their master locks sliding into place halts my steps, my head slamming to the man at my back. "What the fuck do you think you're doing?"

"You cannot stop her. Sir, your fath—"

"Never knew you had a death wish, Kallen. I'm more than happy to help you out with that."

He takes a deep breath, nodding towards the door. "She is fine. Stopping the stream now will only further damage the Vanegas name. You may not like it, but I'm not wrong."

The cart crashes to the floor, making me jerk again towards the screens. Lana's hands shake violently as the man wails. His stomach and chest bubble in nasty burns, burned and charred flesh and blood masking his torso. The air filtration system takes care of the singed smell long before it reaches the ducts. When the blade she picked up slams into his gut, I stare, everyone in the next room too rendered stunned by the sheer brutality of everything that comes next.

Lana screams, making the organ in my chest clench painfully. She shreds him, slashing and stabbing in a frenzy. I see it the moment her blood covered hands slip down the blade, cutting herself. It doesn't slow her down as she vents everything at the now lifeless man. With the heretic's fork fully embedded in his throat, the camera zooms in on his gaping mouth, showing the prongs poking out on the inside. I'm at the control panel in the next second.

"Cut the fucking stream now!" I bellow.

Luca's voice fills the room. "Not yet! They're loving this!"

The sound that leaves me is nothing short of a battle cry as Kallen's hands attempt to jerk me back from the panel.

I see red.

Lana is bloody, and now she's screaming. The sounds are so different from her gentle, delicate demeanor, they inject ice into my veins. They're the type of screams born of agony, years of it. I feel the guilt fully as it settles on my chest, making me work for every breath, something I haven't felt this purely in years.

My fist hits him roughly in the face before I even fully turn, snapping his head back. When he goes down, I follow him, adding another flurry of punches.

I barely hear Lucas' voice, unaware his hand is still on the control. "Fuck, get Jesse down here now!"

My hands wrap around my friend's jaw, slamming his head into the polished floor. "She is mine! The Vanegas name is mine! You will not undermine me again!"

"Sir," he croaks from underneath me. I drive my fist again into his face, knocking him out as I shove to a stand, jerking the master control from beside him.

My eyes land on the tech room, my suit crumpled and bloody as the doors to my room fly open, Jesse panting on the other side. My gun is out of my waistband aimed for Lucas' head. "Cut the fucking stream, or I paint the back wall with your brain."

Immediately, the green light indicating we're live goes red, one of the stunned man's helpers cutting it for him. I don't bother turning to my brother. "Take him to medical. He's not allowed to die."

"Chris—"

"Leave me."

"What has gotten into you, man?"

I take a deep breath, trying to steady myself before I got to her, still not looking at my brother. My brain throbs with the rush of bullshit that floods it. Kill them, myself, her, blow it up. I want her; I want her so fucking badly. I want her to be okay, to be the one who *makes* her okay. I want them all dead, the Sullivans, myself for pushing her into this before she was ready, for not fucking her when she offered. Not holding her tighter, not saving her. Not fucking saving her long before I knew her.

For watching every stream she made and not realizing she was mine.

"She's mine," is all I say before I unlock the doors.

"Okay... The old man is going to fucking—"

"Leave."

I don't look at him, but I can picture his wavy locks as he shakes his head, grunting as he grabs Kallen's hands, tugging him from the room before ordering whoever is guarding outside to help. I wait until the doors shut then open again, someone else retrieving the dead man from earlier. My fists clench as I struggle to control my breathing, control fucking *anything*.

Because Lana isn't screaming anymore, and she isn't asking to be let out. Her stillness sinks into my bones, chilling me from the inside.

16
Nothing

Duality by Slipknot

Christian

When I walk in, Lana doesn't react, her body sagging, her back hunched from the carnage she just wielded and the flurry of emotions that came with it. I approach her like you would a rabid and wounded animal, because I don't do soft.

I don't know how.

Or even if that's what she *needs*.

"Lana, it's done," I say quietly, waiting for some kind of awareness.

She just breathes heavily, her head turned towards the floor underneath the man's feet, to the large pool of blood there like it holds the absolution she needs.

"Princess, talk to me," I order, something oddly akin to panic blooming in my chest.

She doesn't, and when I remove her mask, tossing it to the side, her eyes are empty, entirely unaware. My hands cup her clammy face, sheeted with sweat, forcing those pretty amber eyes to mine.

"Delicate princess…" My voice is harsher than I want it to be, growly. "I'm sorry," I whisper, smoothing my thumb over her lips. They aren't words I've muttered in any meaningful way since the night I apologized to my little sister, my dog, for putting a bullet in his head. I apologized to my father, my mom, maybe even God. All I knew was that I was in pain, that I was sorry. I haven't felt sorry for anything else since, but I'm sorry now.

Still, she doesn't move, and goddamn if I don't feel it in my chest. Deeper than that, if possible, like the very marrow of my being is bothered by the idea of her being bothered. It's fucking stupid, and I can't bring myself to care how illogical my feelings for her are anymore, what they risk.

When I tug her bloody form into mine, she's ramrod straight, but I don't let it stop me. Her hair is silky smooth in my hand as I gather it up, exposing her neck.

"I need you, princess. Come back to me." My lips graze her neck feather light, my tongue darting out to taste her there, her sweet, salty, copper taste exploding on my tongue.

Her breasts push against my chest with each pant, her breath warming the skin beneath my shirt. I want to feel it on my skin. I want all the soft sounds she makes, for her to look at me the way she did in my room. Like maybe, just maybe, I could save her.

"Lana." I say her name like a prayer as my fingers map out the smooth skin on her back, committing it to memory the way I have every other night. This time, my princess isn't sleeping while I worship her. This time, I'm desperate for her to know. My teeth graze her neck. "I should've taken you earlier. I should've slammed you to the bed and forced your pretty thighs apart."

Her panting falters, just a little, her breath coming slower than it was before.

I nip at her flesh, making her jolt. "That's what I wanted to do. I wanted to spread your wet cunt so I could see just how badly you wanted me." My roaming, adoring hands turn possessive, owning, and I couldn't stop them, even if I wanted to. "I want you wrapped around me, crying your sweet little princess tears while I fuck you. You'd cry so pretty on my cock. Tell me, Lana, do you still want me there, between your thighs? Do you want to take my cock?"

Her breath stutters.

"I think you do. All your mean words, your anger, and you're still so desperate to be fucked by me."

I school my features when she shifts closer, pressing into me a little more, her forehead digging into my chest. I don't deserve it, but again, I'm a bastard. When her nails dig into my chest, her small fists clinging to me, I snap. My tender, teasing nibbles turn violent, and I groan heavily as she comes to life, crying out as my teeth latch onto her shoulder, holding her there against me.

"Christian." Her voice is shaky, so fucking soft.

I press harder into her, my hands gathering the silk of her lingerie and ripping the shorts. They come off clean, and my sweet princess begins shaking all over again. When she tries to pull back, her own hands wrenching at my button down within the small space between us, I nearly growl, biting down harder. It's like if I release her now, I'll never get her back. My tongue teases the angry flesh between my teeth, thanking her, tasting her. My hands grip the thin straps of her top, jerking it down over her breasts.

When my teeth pop free, she gifts me a whimper. Her formerly pale cheeks are flushed pink, her pretty amber eyes lidded. She groans as I kneel before her, taking a pebbled nipple into my mouth. Her core rocks, needing friction I won't give her yet. She came back for *me*.

"Please."

Her pleases always hit their mark. How could I not give her everything when she asks so prettily?

My fingers find their way to her soaked core, teasing and prodding at her opening. She's lost to it, her eyes pinching shut as she focuses on trying to catch the spark she needs to implode. Her arousal drips down my fingers, her hands knotted in my hair, trying to guide my mouth lower. As lovely as my princess tastes, I have other plans.

"Christian."

"I'm here, princess, right here." With that, I bite again, my teeth scoring her breast as she cries out. I sink my fingers into her, curling them until her whimpers turn to moans. I watch as the venom bleeds back into her, letting her take what she needs as she fucks herself down on my fingers, grinding her clit against my palm. Her flesh is angry and raised when I release her again, taking a nipple instead. My togue lashes the bud, making her moan, each rough tug she gives me only driving me deeper.

She grinds and moans, takes wildly. Fuck, I can't look away from her, my own cock in a sorry state of need straining against my zipper. The set lights cast her red hair like a fire halo above her head, her breasts heaving as she grinds down. When her body jerks, her mouth parts on a silent scream, coming apart, her arousal soaking my fingers. If I could freeze this moment, I would.

She gasps as I halt my assault on her nipples, extracting my fingers and popping them in my mouth, her sweet, tangy flavor pushing my control harder. Her little tongue darts out, wetting her lips, reminding me sharing is caring.

There's no slow build, no gentle crescendo of need and desire.

My hand captures her jaw, slamming her into me. It's teeth, tongue, and insanity. It's everything.

Lana is everything.

She's mine.

The jacket of my suit hits the ground with the thud, my buttons creating a faint symphony to narrate around it as she tears at my shirt, as desperate for me as I am her. That idea only eggs me on. I don't pull her from me, her togue twirling with mine in a frenzied dance as I jerk the gun from my holster, opening my eyes long enough to aim it at a camera. "Anyone who watches this will be in this room next."

I discard the gun, making quick work of the rest of my clothes. Lana backs away, panting. She's gorgeous, sin personified, her body filling out beautifully with regular meals, her hair shining. When those eyes land on mine, the intermission ends, and my hands grip her waist, the other hiking her leg up, hitching it around my waist.

She gasps as my cock lines up with her entrance, the head teasing her wet slit, her hips shunting as she fights for the tip. I don't give it, though, not yet. Instead, I run my length between her soaked thighs, coating myself in her arousal. My cock weeps, begging to be inside her. "Are you ready for my cock, sweet princess?"

She moans as I line myself up again.

"Words, princess. Tell me how badly you want me to fuck your little cunt."

I need to hear your voice.

"Bad. I need it. I need you to take it."

"Tell me you're mine." I groan past the words, slipping the head of my cock inside her. She's fucking tight, and already, her hips grind down, wanting more, but I hold her steady, my fingers digging into supple flesh.

"Please, please fuck me."

My eyes dart down to the symbol underneath my palm, jealousy flaring in my chest. It flows over before I can get a grip on it. Lana cries out as I bury myself inside her in one violent thrust, her walls clenching around my cock, smothering it in the best way. "Tell. Me. You're. Mine."

I punctuate each word with another thrust, her pretty eyes rolling back in her head, her moans hitting a decimal I hadn't thought possible, merging with screams. "You want... fuck, oh my fucking God."

"Close, but I prefer Christian, princess. Now, tell me you're mine."

Fuck, she feels so good. Her nails score my back and neck, marking me again for her. Her cunt spasms, clinching and gripping me.

"You—" she screams as I grip her other thigh, lifting her up and holding her against me as I pump into her.

"I, what? Belong to you?" What a bizarre time to have butterflies.

"God, God, don't fucking stop," she pleads.

I'll pretend like I could if I wanted to.

"You're not listening, princess." I fuck her harder, her beautiful, palm sized breasts heaving as I move her until her back hits something. Anything. A sick smirk fills my face as I realize it's him. The rigging jostles as I pin my princess to the dead man's chest, grinding my cock around while it's buried to the hilt, catching her clit in the way she needs. If she won't say yes, I'll ensure she can't say no at least. Hearing it from her lips would be preferred, but I'll take what I can get.

For now.

When I reach between us, pinching her nipple, she screams my name, her head pitching backwards to rest on the man's bloody shoulder, her wild red hair tangling in the Heretics Fork. It's only a shade lighter than his blood, and fuck, she's stunning.

"You're really coming all over my cock already? Fucking hell, you are. That's such a good girl, such a good fucking princess."

Her screams dissolve into sobs as she rides out her orgasm. I make quick work, never losing my momentum as I gently untangle her hair from the device.

"I need you to do it again for me."

"No, no, please, I can't."

"You can, and you'll look so fucking pretty while you do it."

She sobs as I wrap my hand around her throat, using it as leverage as I reach over to the scalpel set beside me, the one that always hangs near the rigging. I hold the scalpel blade away from my princess as I grind into the oversensitive nub more. She's begging, pleading, fighting, her cunt soaking my legs, dripping to the bloody floor as she clings to me.

"There you go, princess. Almost there." The words are all growl as they leave me, my cock swelling inside her as my own release surges forward with a vengeance, weeks of having her so close taking its toll.

Fucking Lana was everything I thought it would be and more, so much more. She's sin, death, and deliverance all in one.

She consumes.

I can feel her tightening as I work her over, teasing her nipples and swollen, angry clit until her body freezes again, hurtling towards the edge. My princess is exactly where I need her for what comes next. The moment I still, she cries out, frantically trying to force my cock in and out of her weeping cunt.

I shove her back by the neck, pinning her roughly against him as I lean back, wedging a thigh under her plump ass keeping her up. "You'll want to be still for this."

Her release barrels through her as I let go of her neck, her hands flying out to the rigging to hold herself up, as if I'd drop her.

Never.

She comes so violently, it almost distracts me from the task at hand as I pull her branded skin taut and slide the tip of the blade along her smooth, soft skin. Her cunt spasms as she screams, choking my cock to the point of no return. I follow her over the edge, my teeth digging into my cheek to remain still as she milks me. The blade makes a skilled path around the mark, *their* mark, before I work it underneath, freeing it from her skin.

Lana trembles as I toss the blade across the room, her skin clasped tightly in my hand. The disturbed look on her face is fucking adorable, but she hasn't seen anything yet. I lift the slippery section of skin to my mouth, popping it inside. The tangy copper flavor fills my mouth, the flavor of *her* in her purest form. She's mine, all of her.

Her eyes widen as I chew, the blood from the wound on her hip smearing over me as I'm still lodged deep inside her, where I intend to stay. When I swallow, I'm on her again, my lips claiming hers in a bruising kiss. Her body sags in my arms as I pull her away from the dead man we fucked against. I can't fault her for being slow to respond—I did technically just cannibalize her—but I'd be lying if I said it didn't make me want to lash out, to clip her Achilles tendons and chain her to my bed. Then, my princess surprises me, her small tongue dipping out, tasting mine before she kisses me back, whimpering against my lips. When the kiss breaks, we're both breathless.

"There, princess. Now there's truly no part of you that isn't mine," I whisper as she collapses against me.

My princess didn't get the knight in shining armor who fought honorably to free her from her tower. She got the villain who wrenched her from it, bloody and screaming.

17
Fall

I'm counting her breaths.

Each rise and fall of her blood splattered chest resonates in mine, speaks to me like a fucking prayer. Or an omen, I haven't decided yet. Either way, I clutch my princess tighter as she sleeps, dressed in my suit jacket, the garment swathing her small form, her wounds cleaned and bandaged enough for the night, her eyelids fluttering as she dreams.

"Son."

Fuck.

I halt, my eyes lifting from her towards my father. The press of my gun settles me almost as much as the knowledge that I'd considered using it on him further confirms my omen theory. He lets the cane he's now using, thanks to the sleeping beauty in my arms, take the brunt of his weight for the first time since I can remember, looking tired. Even *that* night, he was distraught, but steady, everything I've been fighting to replicate but never managed.

"She did what was required of her."

"And yet, I've got *another* dead guard on my hands, and my successor clutching a bloody captive like he'll cease breathing the moment he releases her."

Lana stirs, and I make an effort to loosen my grip, not willing to intentionally bruise her too badly until her hip is healed.

Fuck. Fuck. Fucking. Fuck.

I should hand her over, take a vacation, smother myself in cunt and drugs until this passes.

"If you try to take her from me, I will—"

"Enough. I don't plan to wrestle the woman from your arms."

The room swirls for a moment, my eyes narrowing on his dark ones before dropping lower. "Her file." I gesture to the manila folder tucked underneath his arm. He'd had me blocked from the initial report. Of course, I'd just fed what information we had to my own sources, but his were faster. Perks of being the scariest man on the East Coast. For now.

His graying hair is swooped back with the same pomade he's always used, a single clump curling forward on his forehead. "This is what you really want? What you're willing to risk your position as the family head for? Some broken fucking girl from Virgina? God, son, have you any clue what the Sullivans did to her?" He shakes his head. "She was a *good* girl, worked hard for her brother, her mom..." Each word strikes deep as intended, anger bubbling so hot in my chest, I wait for the skin to melt, bubble, and pop. "They had cameras all over that fucking house. They streamed it every single time they raped her. I don't even know if she's aware. Her every moment since that first day was streamed for anyone willing to pay. Hell, the way those bastards would take her, I wouldn't subject a goddamn animal—"

"Enough," I spit, my chest heaving.

"There is no fixing that, Christian!"

"I don't care! I'll wipe out their fucking line, all of them! I'll hunt down every last Sullivan, every fucking man, woman, and child if that's what it takes to stop her pain! I'll make it fucking even if I can't make it okay. I don't give a rancid fuck what it costs me. I don't care how long she cries or if her scars never heal! She chose me! After all those years of pain, it was me she chose to trust, and I will not betray that again. Not for you, not for anything." The last words leave my throat in a growl, all the worst emotions bulleting my chest like wasps, demanding carnage.

My father lifts his chin just as I drop mine, a delicate, shaky hand clenching the front of my jacket, pulling it tighter around her. Lana's eyes are wide, filled with so much fucking pain that it knocks the breath from my lungs. She didn't know. Fucking hell, of course not. I spent the last year of my life dedicated to her, and even *I* didn't find those streams.

I don't look away from her, or her from me, until the sound of my father's cane squeaking on the hardwood forces my eyes to him. He doesn't speak, no small amount of uncertainty there, but when he passes, he smirks, shaking his head as he all but shoves the envelope into my chest. "Whatever you do…"

"Family comes first."

His dark green eyes settle on my princess, but she's beyond seeing again, her pretty golden eyes swimming with unshed tears as she stares at the vaulted ceiling.

"I don't care, Lana. I don't fucking care if you're broken. You're mine."

All at once, it makes sense why he collects the broken ones.

They bend so beautifully.

18
Jacket

Lana

His jacket is huge on me, my fingertips barely poking out of the ends of the sleeves as the room fills with steam. I feel smaller than I have in years. Tiny.

I used to have a dream before the Sullivans, where I would find a man who loved me. He'd be a good husband, sometimes even a father, but I'd get sick. So sick. He'd take care of me, feed me by hand and soothe my failing body. He'd look at me with so much love and adoration, so much sadness, that I would always wake up in tears with the oddest warmth in my chest. I can't count the times in those early years before I was given books or trinkets to fill my time that I sat on my bed, telling the dream to myself out loud, like maybe that would make it something obtainable. That I would die loved.

How many times had someone listened to my story? Watched me cry into my pillow? How many times had I muttered Mom's and Lewis' names out loud?

My eyes look dull. When Christian appears behind me, I nearly jolt, time having slipped at some point.

He's gentle as he frees me from his suit jacket, the fine gray fabric soaked through with blood. I clutch it without thinking, not ready to feel bigger than I am right now. His moss green eyes find mine in the mirror as I cling to it, tears bursting to my eyes with an intensity that makes my mouth gape in a plea I can't give voice to.

Christian lets me keep it.

He's silent as he leads me to the shower, his hands gentle and soothing as he lifts the jacket in places he wants to get wet using the nozzle instead of just taking it off me. The way he washes me mollifies the intense burning on my hip. It's no different than the way Vince and Anton would.

Methodical, soft, thorough. Yet I can't seem to look away from his nude body, the way water drips from his hair to his cheek. He doesn't wipe it away, focused on cleaning me. I almost do, but my arms won't listen. They stay limp at my side as he maneuvers me. My chest aches, but it's a dull, throbbing kind.

I long stopped believing in God, but when my tears break free, I beg him to take me.

Dr. Lamaison, I've decided, is a good man. His thickly accented voice fills the gray room as I lay crumpled on my side, the soaked and bloody jacket now replaced by a hoodie I've never seen before. It smells like Christian, so I clutch it harder in the moments I forget to breathe. I'm exhausted, my eyes heavy, but neither sleep nor God ever take me. My hip is cleaned and bandaged again, stinging like mad. Dr. Lamaison curses quietly. The word fuck seems so out of place on such a proper man, like hearing your pastor drop the f word during mass. He gestures to me, bits and pieces drifting in.

"…shell shock. She's suffering…"

Christian almost looks worried, his deep green eyes keep drifting towards me as he runs his hands through his wet hair, displacing it in a way that looks intentional but isn't. He's just so damn handsome, though, that it doesn't matter. His chest is bare, showing off every chiseled plane. Freckles cover his chest and back. It's cute. I try to find the birthmark that looks like a cloud, but he keeps moving.

"You flayed her skin…"

When my mind becomes mine again, it's Christian's hands that pull me back, his rough knuckles drifting over my thigh absently as he speaks in a hushed, angry tone into his phone. "Get the fucking jet. I want wheels down in Virginia by sunrise."

We're not in Virginia?

I would almost think I keep falling asleep had the effects of exhaustion not been pressing into my skull like a baton, my eyes burning from not blinking.

Christian's boots squeak against the wet tarmac. I'm still wearing the hoodie, now paired with the gray sweatpants someone gave me during my brief stay in my own room. Christian made a deal of it to some small girl who looked close to tears at some point. I can't for the life of me remember the ride here, but I know at some point that sleep did, in fact, take me.

If Christian's arms are tired from hours of holding me, he doesn't show it as he carries me up the narrow stairs to the plane. A bubbly woman appears, offering him a drink and a private show. For a second, something oddly hot bubbles in my chest before it fades. I clutch him harder. Christian shifts me so that I'm straddling his lap, taking the drink and requesting some type of food I don't pay attention to. I've never been on a plane before.

That's not right, though. We aren't in Virginia. I know that's where my family lives, where the Sullivans lived when they were still breathing. Logic tells me he probably took me in one before. I nearly kick myself for missing my first ride in a plane.

He cradles me, now nursing his second drink. The smell of alcohol on his lips should disgust me, fill my chest with panic like it would with them, but they aren't with me anymore, their mark taken by him. The weight of it was profound, even as a new one settled in its place. Pleasure and agony bracketed me as I watched him, transfixed, as he slowly cut the skin away.

Christian stops trying to force feed me when I lift up in his arms, tasting his lips. I'm sure even tainted with bourbon, they are more appetizing than whatever food he's been trying to give me. He doesn't kiss me just like I don't kiss him. He lets me run my tongue over the soft, bowed line. Even as his cock grows underneath me, he just holds me tighter, running his fingers through the hair he brushed.

The next time I awaken, I'm positive sleep finally took hold of me. A small groan slips from my mouth as I stir, my head pounding. My back aches like it does after hours of being settled in a position my spine doesn't approve of, and when I shift my head to the opposite side, it's to a line of passing trees, the gentle engine of an expensive car, and the smell of lemon and leather.

Christian eyes me briefly before turning back to the road, like he's waiting for something. I try to seem as casual as possible as I swipe away the slowly crusting trail of drool decorating the corner of my mouth.

My throat feels like sandpaper, each swallow of my own spit only seems to further irritate it. It takes several attempts at gathering my own saliva in my mouth before I cave. "Water?"

"Center console, princess."

I stare at the passing trees, the nearly empty stretch of highway as I sip the bottle, evading his stares. At this point, he's paying more attention to me than the road, his hand flexing and unflexing on the steering wheel like the anticipation is killing him. I'm not sure what he's expecting from me, so I just watch the trees.

It isn't until the sign for Bedford wizzes past that my lips part, remembering his comment about heading to Virginia. We always took day trips here for the harvest festival. I can almost taste the crisp apples we'd pick, Lewis always reaching for the highest ones, even knowing they were so far out of his reach. When the slight pang in my chest folds in on itself, giving into a searing knife wound, I suck in a ragged breath, clutching the seat belt Christian strapped around me. My eyes slam down to my lap, like that might save me from the reality of my situation.

My face is everywhere, all those men I spent years pleasuring behind a mask, the crimes I committed.

They *have* my face.

Vomit roils up my throat before I can stop it. Thankfully, one panicked look at Christian was all it took. He maneuvers the luxury car to the side of the highway with a skill you'd see in a racing movie, and I fumble with the lock before he's in park, wrenching my car door open just in time to vomit.

There's not much to it, just loud retching that makes my abs hurt and throat burn like hell.

He's there, quiet, gathering my hair and smoothing his rough palm down my back until my body gives up on trying to purge my stomach acid. My mouth gapes to warn him as he steps just barely around where I threw up, crouching to hover above it. His lips render me mute as he kisses me, tenderly, like he's trying to comfort me. When he pulls back, there's not a trace of disgust or irritation on his face.

"Ready?"

I don't nod, just lean back in the car, gripping my bottled water like it's a life preserver as he leans in, the smell of rich bergamot enveloping me as he buckles me in before shutting my door. He's not wearing a suit today; his white t-shirt and dark jeans fit him well. Maybe at some point, he was a normal guy, like maybe at some point, in my crumpled, musty sweats, I'd be normal too. My stomach has settled well enough, my mind drifting to the sweet vendor food Mom used to gush over at each festival as we drive deeper into the heart of Bedford.

My eyes flutter open again as Christian puts the car into park. The trees are naked and bare, all the leaves having long fallen and rotted, Christmas lights dawn the porches of all the quant light colored houses. My eyes find a nativity inflatable that lays limp in the damp grass just down the street. Mom used to put one up like it every year. Even when Lewis's drug addiction took what was left of her, she still plugged it up. It was the only thing she bothered with at that point, having long forsaken the Christmas tree.

It's not until my gaze turns to the beaten-up, tan 2000s Honda accord that my heart stops in my chest, the Jesus fish magnet that still slings to the back bumper tarnished, a car I know for a fact still probably holds a couple dozen of my Lite Brite sticks trapped between the seats.

I open my mouth to speak when another car pulls in behind it, a newer SUV blocking out the beaten Honda. I lurch forward, waiting for a moppy head of blonde hair, the seatbelt locking up at my sudden jolt. When a tall, tanned woman steps out in baby blue scrubs, I sag, my breath leaving me all at once.

I can feel Christian's eyes on me, but I can't bring myself to look away from her as she walks to the door, typing on the phone before shoving it inside the large tote bag she carries. She lets herself into the unfamiliar home, not even bothering to knock.

"Who is she?" I whisper.

Christian shifts in his seat, but I can't take my eyes off the door. "Andrea Carrillo. She's a hospice nurse. Good credentials. Clean record."

My chest cavity bottoms out. Mom had always been so strong, even in her weakest moments, I don't think she ever missed a day of work. Hospice? God, last year, she turned fifty-five.

My hand is on the seatbelt, pressing the release just as a warm, rough hand encases around my wrist, stopping me. The hold is brushing, brokering no questions.

"Christian, I need to—"

"She specializes in end-of-life care."

My heart drops past my stomach and lands on the floorboard by my feet. Lewis shouldn't be doing this alone. He's helping her, right? Clean? He has to be.

For the first time in weeks, I feel the tears that prickle my eyes.

For the first time in weeks, I remember the breeze. My free hand grasps Christian's where it's locked on my wrist, but I don't fight him.

Why did he bring me here?

To let me go?

The thought brings with it a new wave of panic of.... hurt.

When my head snaps to his, my red hair falling wildly in my eyes, he must see it, something dangerously close to adoration in his mossy eyes. I nearly get lost there for a moment. They look so deep, so rich compared to the death winter brings. There's a peace there, a plea that goes unspoken.

Keep me.

His hand tightens seconds before he strips peace from the air. The substance to my soul. The second he kills the breeze.

"She's been taking care of your brother for the past five months."

The silence that fills the car is so profound, not even the rumble of the engine can penetrate it.

"End stage, according to his most recent medical records. The metastatic cancer started in his left arm. Now, it's everywhere. Unresponsive to treatment. He's been on a morphine drip since last month," he swallows hard, only now looking at me, "to keep him comfortable."

My fist collides roughly with his face, drawing on everything that is *her* as I rage against him. It's not a small crack that breaks the dam—it's a fucking bomb. My heart shatters, mixing with the perfectly vacuumed carpet on the floorboard. The gore seeps underneath the soles of shoes I don't recognize as I hit Christian. I claw, smack, and punch, tears coating my face as sobs rack my chest. I kick and retch until I find my words.

"*They need me!*"

His hands band around mine, shoving them onto his chest, where I feel his heart raging inside. "*I need you, Lana!*" A strangled, broken sound escapes me as he releases my wrists, gripping my face. "They left you! Never even filed a missing person's report. They. Never. Looked!"

His words should shake me, but they don't. My tears burn my eyes, but I don't dare remove my hands from his chest, my single remaining anchor. "I wasn't missing! They knew exactly where I was!"

His eyes widen for a second before the narrow venom swallows his mossy green irises. I want to drown in it, to be swallowed, burned alive by the pure contempt I see there. "They knew the entire time."

The scoff I make is an ugly sound, not at all the breeze. "Of course, that was the fucking deal. His debt, his *life,* for me. I gave it willingly!"

I turn away so hard, my head knocks against the passenger window, avoiding the disgust on his face as I watch the door. My sobs fill the cabin of the car with a bitter agony no amount of detailing will get out.

When my hand claps on the door handle again, it's the weight of his hand on my thigh that stops me. "I *can't* let you go, but I give you my word... you'll never see that room again. Lana... please. I don't deserve you, but you're *mine*. I need you. I don't care if it breaks us both."

The earnest, tortured sound of his voice makes me sob harder.

19
New

I sobbed, raged, and bargained with him until the sun peaked in the sky. Once it started to dip, I grew silent. Nothing filled the car but his soft touches and gentle warnings when I tried to get out. It gets dark so early this time of year, and you could barely see the snow as it started to spit unless you stared at the streetlamps. This time, when he puts the car in drive, I don't fight it. No more sobs tear at my raw throat. No more bargaining or pleas. My place isn't here.

The Sullivans made sure of it.

Or maybe it never was.

Maybe there's no more use for the breeze.

When I lean over the center console, resting my head on my arm, I sleep.

"Princess, I would let you rest, but we're already late." The warmth of the voice is only second to the hands making gentle, adoring passes on my face, lovingly tracing my features like the husband from my dreams. I grumble, tucking my face into the bend of my arm to escape the featherlight touch, my head still pounding. "Sweet Lana, they're waiting for us."

My heart stills, my head coming up so quickly, the cabin of the car spins. "Mom and Lewis?" My voice is hoarse.

He nearly cringes. "No..."

I rub my eyes, fishing out the crust before wiping it on my dirty sweatpants. The dash on the car only says it's a little after seven, but the darkness of the small parking lot screams midnight, the snow now falling in billows. I don't ask what he means, but I accept the hesitant kiss he presses to my cheek before he exits the car. His dark waves catch the snowflakes as if they're christening him. My head is light as he opens my door, unbuckling me, his smell swirling around me as his warm breath fights against the cold.

The warm light from inside the small church disagrees with my somber mood and the growing snowstorm as he ushers me from the car and across the small lot. It's only now I recognize the armed men in tactical uniforms posted up in the dark, each one looking fit to go to war and widely out of place in the small Baptist church in Bedford, one Mom would always set up little picnics at so we could binge all the vendor food we hoarded from the festival.

If I hadn't long given up the faith I was raised in, I would shrink under the warring stare of the local pastor as he greets us. When he casts a pained, sympathetic look my way approaching me with arms open, it's the dark presence at my side that stops him. Christian's eyes are endless pools of deep green, his jaw clenched as he towers over the older man. When the man's own jaw tightens, it's clear he's battling with something. His mouth is barely open when Christian ends the standoff.

"I trust you've had time to prepare."

A stream. My eyes prickle, my chest finding a way to cave in deeper. It's a wonder the organs are working at all.

The older man stares at me, wringing his hands before a guard at his back. One with a badly busted face flicks the safety off his assault rifle, giving the man a light tap with the barrel. He nods once, and I know the war he was fighting is over.

"Yes…" he gestures to the room behind him. "All your… documents were in order." My heart lurches for the man when he takes a sudden step forward. The room comes to life around us, his hands cupping my face. "God is with you, child."

My lips part.

Christian mumbles something under his breath, shoving the man's hands off me. "Enough." His voice is nearly demonic, surrounded by holy pictures, warm tones, and pews that have been absorbing tears and prayers since before I was alive.

Christian's warm hand on the small of my back grounds out the brief panic the pastor's words infected me with as he steers me down the aisle, the guards staying back. When we reach the pulpit, Christian's hold on me changes from a warm guide to a *lock*, a warning vice around my wrist, his fingers digging into and bruising the flesh. My heartbeat kicks up as I glance at him, then the pastor walking around us with a sullen, almost ashamed look on his face. When he speaks, he doesn't face me, the bible in his hands shaking as he stands before us.

"Dearly *beloved*, we are gathered here in the presence of God to witness a… *joyous* occasion: the union of Lana Porter and Christian Vanegas in Holy Matrimony."

The blood whooshing to my head makes me sway on my feet, and Christian only grips me tighter, tugging me to his side. "What? Christian…"

His jaw clenches, his fingers making languid, testing passes, daring me to say no.

The pastor's voice grows thick, his wrinkled eyes glossing over. "The sacred covenant of marriage is a sanctuary and a home. It must not be entered into lightly, but reverently, discreetly, soberly, and advisedly, with God's guidance and blessing."

Sick builds again in my stomach as I take a step back, and Christian tenses further at my side. "Careful, princess. You'll wound me."

"I can't—" I scoff, my head swirling. "Why are you doing this?"

When his dark eyes turn on me, I realize the sick feeling in my gut is morphing. It's a fluttering now, a deadly one. He gives me a devastating smile, one his eyes betray, showing his nerves. "You're mine Lana, I told you that. I absolved you of their hold, told you I needed you, that I wanted to keep you. Those words were not spoken lightly. When I consumed your flesh, it was a sacrament. *My vow.* I only mean to make it legally binding."

"Christian..."

He cups my face, slamming his lips to mine, and I'm lost to him. I whimper as he consumes me, his tongue demanding entry, and I give it to him. God help me, my soul is dying, left in tatters, and I give him what's left of it. When he pulls away, his heated eyes burn me from the inside.

"If my words are not enough to convince you, I will drag members of his congregation out here one by one. I'll lodge a bullet in their skulls for each time you deny me."

The pastor makes a choked sound, his whole-body trembling. I feel my cheeks flush as I turn back towards him, my hands shaky as I try to smooth out my dirty sweatpants.

"You make a *stunning* bride," Christian offers, his arm locking me in place again.

But I... I'm not leaving.

"We rejoice today as Lana and Christian receive one of God's greatest gifts: a loving partner to grow with, to share life's joys and challenges, to build a family, to grow old with, to journey with in faith throughout all of their days. "So let us pray, asking for His blessing on this marriage."

The pastor's tears plop onto his open bible.

Hope is a funny thing...

"Oh, Heavenly Father, bless this couple—"

Christian shifts. "Skip the prayer. We all know you don't mean it." I glance up at him, my flush creeping down my neck when he frowns, like he just remembered I was there. "Unless you wish to hear it, princess."

I shake my head.

"Lana, have you come here freely and without reservation to marry?" he asks, and one of the guards snickers behind us.

The man sputters, his hands fumbling with the pages of the bible, snot dripping from his nose. "Right. I, uhm. My apologies."

He continues to flounder, and I don't know what possesses me, only that I've endured enough pain today. I don't have the stomach to sit through more. When I step forward, much to the displeasure of Christian, I place my shaking hands on his cold, mottled ones, stilling them.

"Lana," Christian warns, but I ignore him.

The pastor's eyes meet mine, fear in them that I know well. I give him a weak smile that doesn't touch either of us. "I have."

Christian's voice sounds thick when he clears his throat. "Come back, princess."

I give the man a small nod before stepping back into Christian's arms. The pastor steals himself once again, sniffling.

"Do you take Christian Vanegas to be your husband, to love him, comfort him, honor and keep him in sickness and in health, and forsaking all others, be faithful to him as long as you both shall live?"

I suck in a shuddering breath, the bandage on my hip pulling painfully as Christian goes rigid. He's... actually nervous. It's almost... sweet. "I do."

"Christian, have you come here freely and without reservation to marry?"

"I have."

"Do you take Lana to be your wife, to love her, comfort her, honor and keep her, in sickness and in health, and forsaking all others, be faithful to her, as long as you both shall live?"

My heart thunders in my chest.

"I do."

The pastor pauses, looking at us. "Do you have vows?"

I panic, my mouth opening and closing. I'd thought about this moment so many times, played it over in my mind as a child, but now, everything is empty.

Christian's eyes find mine without hesitation, dark hair falling into his face, bottom lip swollen from where I hit him just hours ago. "I will spend the rest of my days worshipping you, protecting you, earning my right to be your husband, my *right* to your trust."

Tears prickle my eyes, and all I can offer is a nod.

When the time to exchange rings comes, panic once again swarms me until Christian wipes it away, placing a delicate moss agate ring on my finger. It fits perfectly, the light green gem standing proud on the thin sliver band. My fingers are fumbling, my palms slick with sweat as I return the favor with his own thick silver band.

"Lana and Christian, having witnessed your marriage vows in the eyes of God and before... *all* who are assembled here, by the authority invested in me by American Marriage Ministries and the State of Virgina, I pronounce you husband and wife. You may now kiss the bride." With that, he sags, turning away from us to rest his head on the back wall.

I barely notice his distress, because within a second, I'm swept up in Christian's arms, a yelp leaving me as he hooks my thighs around his hips, his mouth greeting mine halfway. What little space there is between us fizzles, igniting in my veins as I deepen the kiss, the tenderness in my core and the burning, pulling pain at my hip forgotten as he claims me.

He only breaks the kiss long enough to utter a single word. "Out."

The room clears of all but one, and I nearly feel guilty now that the mind-numbing sadness isn't as profound. I can hear the cries from the back room behind the stage where I know his congregation is being held.

"This... this is a house of God. Have you not defiled it enough?" the man seethes, his head turned towards the heavens.

"Then let God witness our consummation," Christian purrs in my ear as I fail to stifle my answering moan.

20

Vanegas

Closer by Nine Inch Nails

Somewhere between his hoodie being wrenched over my head and my musty sweatpants being jerked down over my ass, I realize if Christian asked me to follow him into hell, *I would.*

If he asked me to help him drag each congregant out and introduce them to the violence and misery that chokes me…with tears in my eyes, *I would.*

My hands grip the back of the pew as he has me kneel on the seat, his lips peppering each notch in my spine with kisses. I can feel them deeper than the surface of my skin, as if he's touching past the vertebrae and into the sinew and meat—a kiss, an itch I'll never be able to rub out. I suck in a breath as he reaches my ass, his tongue dipping out to taste the sensitive skin linking my core to my asshole.

"Relax, princess. I will never take you here." The words are a growl, menacing.

Instead of embarrassment, my eyes again burst with tears. My nails dig into the built-up wax on the pew, leaving little crescents in their wake, a gratitude I can't swallow past clogging my throat. When I bend, my forehead knocking into the pew, emotion I've spent years refusing to feel threatens to drown me. It's his tongue that helps me surface. My breath is robbed from my lungs as his tongue finds my already wet slit, lapping at it with slow, methodical strokes. He spreads me further, careful of my still-healing ass, his tongue seeking out my clit. He sucks it between his teeth, making me buck, the pressure too much all at once. When pain borders too close to pleasure, his hands pave their way up my sides, his fingertips tickling me, leaving goosebumps in their wake.

"Christian…" I plead, my clit still held captive between his teeth, his tongue teasing it.

He groans against me, giving the swelling nub an extra flick of his tongue.

He's saying wait.

But I can't

I've waited years for him.

My knight in shining armor.

"I need you."

His fingers find my nipples, teasing and flicking. I'm moaning, bucking into his mouth, blind to the way my bandage is pulling free from my skin, the warmth of my own blood coating my hip. Christian pinches my nipples at the same time as he releases my clit, lavishing it in tiny circles, and light explodes behind my eyes, the scream leaving me guttural. He wields the pain I've grown accustomed to, the pleasure I chase expertly.

"Fuck, you are perfection, sweet Lana. All mine."

"Yes, yours," I pant, my head reeling from the violent and sudden climax. I'm grappling, but he's already pulling me up into him. My legs are weak, blood running down my leg again, but I don't care as I work his t-shirt over his head. My heart is racing in my chest as I look up at him, asking permission.

His smile is everything, and I don't waste a second.

My lips trail over his chest, the scars there, wondering when he got them, vowing I'll memorize every story one day. My tongue teases over his nipples. When I go to kneel, my hands working to open his belt, he catches me. "I'll let you explore my cock with that pretty mouth another night, princess."

Princess. That name should fill me with resentment, hate. Maybe even fear.

Yet, every time he says it, my stomach fills with butterflies.

He backs me up the small stairs on the stage, leading me to a long table laid out before the large crucifix suspended on the wall. It's cold on my back as he lays me out, spreading me open. "I was worried you wouldn't want me."

I freeze on my mission to remove his pants, so he takes over. My eyes snap to find his on my chest, not meeting mine, and it's not until his brows knit together that he does. The vulnerability in his deep green depths hits me like a ton of bricks, and for a second, I believe him without reservation, forgetting everything that brought me here. "And if I had?"

His teeth snap together, venom filling his voice. "I would've slaughtered everyone in this church and then implored you to reconsider. My sweet, sweet Lana. I stole you from your tower, but you had claimed me long before I met you."

I scream for friction as he rubs his daunting length up and down my slit, covering himself in my arousal. "You were a fan?"

"I was obsessed with you. It was out of necessity at first. You and those cunts were ruining my life's work. Then, you stumbled on your way back to the SUV. You were... delicate, awkward, *sweet. You were mine*."

I gasp as he sinks the head of his cock inside me, bobbing there for a moment despite the clenching of his jaw, the restraint it's taking him to draw this out plastered on his taut muscles. "And when we return to your home? What's changed?" I gasp, desperately trying to bear down, needing to be filled by him despite my blood now slicking the table underneath me.

The smile he grants me is nothing short of sinister as he leans down, kissing the tender area just beside where he cut me. "For Vanegas, family is forever. Family comes first, always." He moans as he runs his tongue through the blood, dragging it up towards my navel. "So I made you family, and when I pump your pretty little cunt full, and your stomach swells with my child," my core tightens, desire making my version blurry as he licks his lips, "neither you, the Sullivan line, nor the full force of the Vanegas wrath could tear me from you. This..." He leans up, towering over me like a god. *My god.* "This is forever. Even if I'm long rotted in the ground, you will carry the Vanegas legacy. There will be no other for you, no other for me, *wife.*"

With that, he buries himself inside me, and I watch Christ—*my husband* unravel. He grasps my hips, careful of the damaged skin, lifting them off the table as he makes good on his words. Every vow, he pounds into my flesh. I'm a leaf dancing on the ocean, at his mercy as he fucks me. The roll of his hips is long and deep, hitting something inside me that leaves me desperate, whimpering. My mouth gapes to tell him, to beg maybe, but my voice fails, so I settle for showing him.

I'll be worthy of the Vanegas name. There's no going back for me either—only forward, and I choose him every bit as much as he chooses me, whatever that means.

I'm not ready to say goodbye to the breeze, but one day... I will be.

My nails score his skin as I claw my way up to him until he's holding me, his cock still plunging into me relentlessly, sending me to levels I'd never achieved. Our skin slapping together fills the chamber, the stained-glass bearing witness to our need. His hand knots in my hair, forcing my head back. "You want me to stuff your cunt full of my cum?"

"Yes. Please."

"Tell me then, princess, what should I do?"

"Fuck…" I gasp, grinding down on him, my blood making us slide together. "Fill me up. Please."

"My filthy princess."

"Yes, God, oh fuck, I'm gonna—"

"Not yet," he growls before he sits me back on the table, my legs wrapped around his waist as he thrusts into me. "Fuck, look at you, taking my cock so well."

My teeth score my inner cheek, trying to fight past the orgasm threatening to rip me to shreds. Tears spring to my eyes, soaking down my cheeks as waves of pleasure bracket me. I lean forward, letting my clit grind against him as he moans my name, his cock rubbing a place inside me I didn't know existed.

This is every bit as overwhelming as it was in that room, but somehow more. So much more.

"Please!" I cry out.

"Desperate little princess, I can't deny you anything."

I scream, hitching forward as his thrusts become soul shattering, jerky. He finds his own release as I bite into his chest, my tears and blood soaking his skin. My hands tremble as I run my fingers through my blood, smearing it up his chest, onto his beautiful face, and when I brush his lips, they fall open, licking my fingers clean.

When he dresses me again, carrying me out into the already warm, waiting car, I'm languid in his arms. *I'm his.*

21
Family

Christian

My newlywed bliss was short-lived.

It wasn't at any fault of Lana's, but the dumb cunts who held her. Well, their family line, at least. I can't say I blame the oil typhoon. His son's countryside home gets raided, they manage to get themselves murdered for running a snuff operation on the grounds, kidnapping and holding a woman hostage for four years, computers wiped, house in flames. Not to mention, they'd managed to become enemies of a notorious crime family. I'm sure that would be a hard enough pill to swallow, a reason to run and bury your head in the sand.

As anyone with half a brain cell would do.

Only he didn't account for *me*.

For how far I was willing to go to right a wrong.

He didn't expect his sisters, all six of them, to be hunted down. If it hadn't made *daddy cunt* bunker down in full *oh shit* mode, I would smile. If I were a better man, I would consider it a debt paid, but my sweet Lana, she shed a lot of tears at the hands of his sons, so I have more work to do.

Even if I only took a family member for every time they forced themselves on her, the debt would remain unpaid long after the Sullivan line was gone.

"Are you listening to me?" Jesse barks from beside me.

"Not even remotely."

"You're needed at the Hallum site! They've been running extra streams, pulling protocol. They're going to catch the eyes of the authorities and—"

I round on him, stopping our descent on the stairs. "When exactly were you going to tell me?"

"Oh, you mean why didn't I magically teleport to wherever the fuck you moseyed off to in the dead of night with the Blood Princess in tow? Why didn't I show up like a little messenger pigeon when your phone was off for forty-eight hours? Or when you got home, with my new sister-in-law—*can't believe you didn't invite me to your fucking wedding by the way*—and I had to start damage control because there was a very scared pastor and a room filled with at least ten families all found tied up in a random church in Virgina? At what point, Christian should—"

"You did take care of that, yes?"

Jesse throws up his hands. "Of course I did. I always take care of it." I stare at him as he runs his hands down his face. "Father isn't going to like you taking her as your wife. I hope you have a plan, Christian. Family comes—"

"She is family," I growl, heading back down the stairs.

"He wants the Hallum site cleared by tomorrow, asshole!"

I shake my head, jerking up my phone to check the cameras. I'd managed to delay the news of our arrival for three days, but nothing stays hidden for long.

"And I'm still pissed about the wedding! I could've written a speech!"

Lana is standing in front of the window, her arms crossed tightly around her like it's the only thing keeping her together. If you saw her from outside, I'm sure she'd look like a ghost. I've spent my last few days caring for her, fucking her, making her as comfortable as possible, but still, there is a barrier between us, one I'd laid the groundwork on. I'm not the kind of man who can chip away at it, who can give her space and time. No, if there was a barrier, I'd obliterate it. I'd smother her, force her to see all the reasons why she can smile.

And now, I have to leave.

A few hours away seems like too long, but I refuse... and Father is ready to load ammunition on why bringing her in was a mistake. I won't risk her going with me, not when she's so... delicate. Hurting. It'll take time for her to see this place as a home. She's not locked away, but she refuses to leave our room all the same. She's safe. We have accounted for two out of the three Sullivan brothers' corpses, the third presumed buried underneath what's left of the estate. My deep breath does nothing to calm my nerves, so I lock my phone and head back up the stairs.

Back to her.

Work can wait.

"Son."

I should've lived off compound.

I open my mouth to tell him to fuck off when he gestures towards his wing. "My office."

The sides of my phone dig into my palm as I squeeze, careful not to crack the screen.

"I'll be quick," he offers, shaking his head before turning towards the second landing hall, his cane pressed into the runner on the landing.

When you enter my father's office, you're always hit with the thick layer of the incense he burns. Looking at Aurelio Vanegas, burning incense, meditation, and crystals wouldn't even cross your mind. Yet, here we stand, in a very expensive professional-looking smoke shop. I remove my shoes as he does, sitting them on the rack before shutting the wide double doors behind us. He doesn't waste any time making me consider committing war crimes against him.

"Why is the Halum site still active?"

I walk to his serving cart, pouring myself a stiff glass of bourbon. "Perhaps because I was only made aware Halum was an issue a few moments ago."

His cane rests against the side of his desk as he glares at me, his dark eyes creating a black hole in the side of my head. "If you're having trouble managing—"

"I'll have it handled before the end of the night."

"And the princess? Her last stream was a work of art. The viewers enjoyed the raw show of emotion. If she can keep that up, the mess you made at the Sullivan compound might just be worth it, not to mention the mess you continue to make where that family is involved."

The bourbon burns my throat as I toss it back. "There won't be another stream."

"You've lost your fucking mind. You sample her cunt one time, and—"

The thick, intricate glass hits the cart harder than I meant for it to, cracking the base. "Watch the way you speak about my *wife*."

His eyes widen for a moment before narrowing. It's not often you can surprise my father. If I was any less pissed, I'd savor it. "You really have lost your mind, then."

"You assume I ever had it."

That pisses him off? Good. Now we're playing on the same level.

He surges up from the desk, his fist slamming down hard enough to send his crystals scattering to the floor. Not very *Zen* of you, father. "I told you—" he bellows, but I cut him off, stalking forward until my thighs meet the opposite side of his desk less than an arm's length between us.

"*You* told me family comes first. Since that day, I have honored it to a fault. I have bled for this family! Now, she will be a part of it."

"She will perform. We needed her!"

"The Blood Princess is dead! If she sets foot in that room again, your empire will burn, and I will light the fucking match. Would you truly have *your* daughter-in-law broken, half naked and forced to perform in your shows? And when she is pregnant with your grandchild, you would have her under that duress?"

"She is pregnant?" he asks, leaning back.

"Maybe. If not now, she will be soon. Lamaison said she should have no issue carrying."

He shakes his head, falling heavily into his seat, and I do the same in mine. "Then this was your plan from the beginning, was it, son? To take our golden ticket for yourself?"

"One of many plans; that's what you taught me. And spare me the golden ticket bullshit—you're a greedy old man. I did what I set out to do: stop the Sullivans from encroaching on our territory. *She* was never part of the long term. You don't need her!"

"What about the Vanegas legacy? What she could have meant for your place at the head?"

I shake my head. Already, my temples are pounding. "The blood princess is a myth, a legend. A *masked* woman..."

"You mean to replace her?"

"I mean to leave it up to my *wife* how she wants the legend to end. The hell she suffered—"

He waves a hand, steepling his fingers before resting his forehead against them. "Jace has been working to ensure there are no remnants of the streams that show her face. They were never downloadable. The

Sullivans had malware in place to avoid recordings being made, but you already know this, I assume?

I nod, shifting in my seat. "Have him double check. I want it as if it never happened."

"He's already on his third pass."

My hair is still slightly damp from the shower I took at our in-home gym. My suit is suddenly tight and scratchy. The knot in my chest formed from the uncertainty of Vince Sullivan lessens knowing my father was already looking out for her.

When I stand to leave, I'm halfway out the door when he stops me. "She will be safe while you are in Hallum, son, and every day after."

I nod at him before heading into the hall, the organ in my chest feeling full again for the first time since that night.

22
Found

Lana

I nestle my head into Christian's chest as he holds me, his hand making gentle passes up and down my spine. A glance at the clock tells me he's already late. He should've left for the other snuff location an hour ago.

I'm in New York, apparently.

"You should go," I mumble before promptly reburying my face in his chest, hating everything about him being gone. It's not that him leaving for a few hours is the worst thing. No, it's the distance that had me passing on dinner and nausea swirling in my gut. Even the orgasms he just gave me barely took the edge off my growing anxiety.

"Already getting tired of me, princess?" he coos, but I don't miss the way his hands halt their gentle passes to wrap around my waist instead. Deep down, I think my terrifying, adoring husband wants to be needed too, even if my being here, being with him, didn't start consensually.

If my chest wasn't still a gnarly, festering wound, I would smile. Instead, I push up, ignoring the painful pulling from my hip and the wrapped cut on my hand as I rest my forehead on his. "You'll come back, right?"

It's a whisper, and I hate how vulnerable it feels to say it out loud, how stupid I feel for even asking.

"*Nothing*, Lana, *nothing* would keep me away."

I watch with barely suppressed panic as he dresses, refusing to wash my arousal off his cock until he returns. His dark hair is even more tousled than usual, thanks to the sex we just had. It looks...*devastating* on him. For a moment, a wave of insecurity washes over me, my eyes dipping towards the updated wardrobe, now fully stocked with designer clothes for me.

Clothes.

No lingerie.

I never want to wear lingerie again.

He didn't buy any.

My bedroom growing up could fit inside, with room to spare. The opulence I've been surrounded by the last few years never really occurred to me. Sure, I hadn't been blind to it, but it just seemed...irrelevant, another byproduct of my circumstances. I'd never...noticed.

I shrink against the ottoman I pushed against the window, trying and failing to tear my eyes from my husband as he straightens his suit jacket. Like this, he looks like any other suited up man in a luxe menswear catalog. Like this, you'd never know how dangerous he is, how...wild what's inside him is. I guess the same could be said about me.

Except people do know. Lewis and Mom...they know what I became. The Sullivans sent them the link in those early days, one for the twenty-four-hour stream. I haven't taken a full breath since Christian told me.

I shut my eyes, pleading for that train of thought to pass. I immediately regretted asking Christian to tell me everything when we got back; I wasn't ready. God, I would never be ready. Still, I didn't stop him. I watched him pass through every emotion I should've: rage, grief, sadness even towards the end, and none if it could break past the panic or the whooshing in my ears.

I couldn't even manage to be angry, although Dr. Lamaison assured me it would come, that I would break past this moment. I hadn't said a word while he patched me up again. Good to know my current miserable existence is that obvious. My silence was at least half worry that Christian would hurt him if I spoke, but he seems...more relaxed, like our marriage, however unconventional, had calmed him a bit. My acceptance of it had given him an answer he needed. My knight in shining armor, for all his insanity, had needed to know I wanted him too. He wanted me to choose *him*.

Christian grips my chin, gently angling my head towards him. "I will be back soon." I watch his jaw clench and unclench before he releases me, reaching into his pocket, pulling out his phone. My eyes widen as he presses it into my hands. "This is for you; my number is already programmed into it, as is the number for my second in command. If, for any reason, you don't get me, call him. Kallen is a little banged up right now, so he's been taking a few days off, but he's a good guy and he's close. He wouldn't hurt you—unless I told him to."

I roll my eyes at that, and the smile he gives me almost forces one to my face.

When his lips find mine, the weight of the phone lessens, the wound in my chest muted for a moment. Christian takes a step closer, his knee finding its way between my legs as he leans into me, deepening the kiss. Our only barrier is my pajama pants and tank top, and even that feels too thick. He tastes like mint, bourbon, and *me*, a heady flavor that makes my head spin. It lasts all of ten seconds before he walks out the door, leaving it open, an invitation. Two men flank the opening just after he passes the threshold, both careful not to look inside. I can see guns on their sides as I walk up to close the door, my breath leaving me in unsteady pants by the time I reach the window.

I lasted an hour and a half before the gray walls felt like they were closing in on me, the cellphone gripped tightly in my hand. I'm not sure if he realizes the choice he gave me. One call, and it ends. Sure, I'll spend the rest of my life in prison, but... maybe I can do the right thing, give some peace to those left from the lives I took.

My body shakes so hard, my teeth chatter as I unlock the screen, going for the Dialpad. The moment the wallpaper pops up, my brain shuts down, the shaking halted by a moment of shock.

Christian's face stares back at me, the corners of his green eyes tilted up, reflecting his smile. I'm laying behind him on the bed, flipping through one of his books, oblivious to him, to the world. It all seems so... normal, like we're just a husband and wife, like I wasn't reeling after four years of torment, like I wasn't a serial killer.

Like my little brother, the reason for all of it, isn't on his deathbed.

Like he and Mom hadn't washed their hands of me.

I yelp as the phone dings, a text message coming through, sending the phone crashing to the ground. My head goes light as I nearly dive off the ottoman, snatching it off the floor, a flurry of aches ricocheting throughout my body.

The Knight is what he saved his number as.

My heart thrums heavily in my chest.

The Knight: If you make that call, princess, it changes nothing. You'll be mine, no matter where you are, and I will hold no guilt over the lives I take to get you back.

My breath leaves me in a rush, my head snapping up, as if I'll be able to find whatever camera he has hidden in here. I shouldn't be surprised—of course he's watching me. If I were him, I would too. I just…is it only him?

I tug the phone to my chest, trying to steady my breathing, when it dings again.

The Knight: I would sooner cut off my own cock than share the sight of you, in case you were wondering.

My lips tug up, just a little.

Me: Are you safe?

The Knight: I'll be home by morning. Sweet dreams, princess.

Me: Am I allowed to leave the room?

The Knight: It's your home. Anything in my wing is open to you. The west wing is my father's. North belongs to Jesse, and South is staff. Don't make me kill my brother or the staff. The men at your doors will show you anywhere you want to go. Anything on the sublevel is off limits without me for now.

I lock the phone, placing it face down in my lap, my eyes trained on the door. I had free rein in the Sullivan mansion too, so long as Jax never caught me out alone, but closing myself off in my room gave me a sense of peace. I wouldn't have made it had I known…

I'm up from the seat, jerking things down from the closest, my eyes burning. I'm out the door before I can think better of it, before I can rationalize the stupidity of my actions. The guards at the door don't react as I burst through it like a crazy person. When I turn, fists balled, ready for the consequences of my actions, they give me a small nod before refocusing forward.

This isn't the Sullivans.

I'm not there.

They are dead. Dead.

I replay their deaths in mind, like I have thousands of times since that day, over and over, letting them soothe the worst of my frazzled nerves.

The gurgling sound Anton made as the tool embedded in his throat, whirling and shredding, a far cry from the way he'd drunkenly laugh as he choked me.

Vince's shocked, pained face as I tossed the acid at him. The way he yelled was nothing like his cool, calm demeanor, one that made him so easy to trust in those first few days…until he showed me his… age preferences, his collections that made me vomit.

And Jax.

He shrieked. He begged. How many times had *I* begged? How many times did *I* do everything he wanted? I was well behaved, went out of my way, and yet he took me savagely. He'd keep going until my legs buckled and my begging went silent.

I'm with Christian now.

The Vanegas.

I'm a Vanegas.

Another hour or two passes as I explore. I'm not particularly going in any direction, just wandering. The *house*, if you can call it that, is framed in thick wood that's probably older than me, elaborate stairwells, molding, carpets, and tapestries decorating the halls and rooms. The décor screams Mediterranean, rich colors and smelling like incense I can't see, but the house itself stands as a beacon of English Tudor style. It's nothing like the gaudy, polished Sullivan mansion. I could almost believe this is someone's… *home.*

When my wandering leads me down a wrought iron spiral staircase, I gasp at the room below me. It's like stepping into a well-curated terrarium: the large sunroom is overflowing with exotic plants, all encasing a recessed living area. Snow and ice batters the floor-to-ceiling windows, but it feels like summer. The men who have been shadowing my journey fidget behind me, but I ignore them.

I rub absently at the wound in my chest, trying to soothe it as I head to one of the many windows, scooting onto a huge burnt orange bean bag type chair. The smell of incense increases, the built in aqueduct system trickling nearby. It's like stepping into one of the ambiance YouTube videos I used to have to fall asleep to.

It's crazy how you adapt. Five years ago, I would stay up all night, tossing and turning, without one of those videos.

Suddenly, I didn't need it, like my brain decided to shut that part down to better handle more pressing matters. Suddenly, a year in, I developed a pain tolerance I never had before. I was able to eat food I hated because none of it had flavor. I was able to stop my tears and not feel when it suited me. I was able to hate The Blood Princess, feel insurmountable guilt, to keep track, and still…get excited when they lead me to that room. I was able to enjoy the rape. Even the most painful ones offered mental stimulation, if not orgasms. I adapted without ever meaning to.

Maybe I could again. I could learn to breathe past the pain in my chest. I could find my anger and, someday, peace. I stare at the large garden covered in a blanket of snow and ice, wondering if anyone would ever need the breeze again. My face is hot and wet from my tears, but this feels like a good place to cry.

"Some people believe plants, like crystals, can absorb emotions."

I jump, my head snapping over my shoulder to the large man now reclining on the deep blue leather sofa in the lower level of the recessed living space. Christian's father discards his cane beside him, his hands folded in his lap, and I clear my throat as I frantically wipe at my tears with the long sleeves of the baggy athletic top I grabbed earlier.

"That's why I always loved this place. A human, like a plant, can't thrive if it's being forced fed all the wrong things. It takes time, patience, to grow."

My eyes slam to my lap as his raise to meet mine. "I'm sorry, sir, about your knee."

He laughs, and the sound is so warm, damn near jolly, that it takes me aback. "I can't blame you for defending yourself. Sometimes, I lose track of decorum when I have a goal in mind."

My throat burns as I swallow. "Is that what this is? You're here because you want me to perform?"

When he groans to a stand, his tailored robe coat fastened in the front, I remember it's well into the night. My hands fist the loose fabric of the seat, trying to remember what pocket I put the phone in.

"Nobody told me how terrible children are before I had eleven of them. How their adorable toothy smiles would turn into grown-ups one day. That they would smile less, and I would waste time wondering if it was my fault." He leans down, grabbing some kind of metal spray bottle. I watch him tentatively grasp a large leaf of a fern, studying the stem before spraying it with the water. His lack of an answer has me fighting for the phone, panic clawing up my chest.

"I always told my children that family comes first, but no one took it to heart quite like Christian. He had his reasons." His thumb runs over his badly scarred fingers. "He made you family. Know that your place here, although not...favorable for you at first, will be, if you let it. We are not Sullivan scum, but we're not... *good* people. The quicker you come to terms with it, the easier it will be for you here, Lana."

The sound of my name makes my throat clog further. God, I feel so stupid for crying in front of him.

"I will not have any daughter of mine in danger, so your days of performing are done. As a Vanegas, you must fill the space you left.

Protect and serve your family when you are ready. It will be your responsibility to train a replacement, to prepare her. You have the backing of my family, the support while you heal." He half laughs, stepping forward, making me flinch despite not feeling like I'm in danger.

"My son will ensure that their lineage pays for what was done to you. He's been working tirelessly to clear any trace of your identity from the web. We all have. I'll let the man himself tell you what else he's been up to but know that you have a family now. You are not alone." He laughs again, less bitter this time as he scratches his salt and pepper hair. "Whether you want to be or not."

My mouth opens and closes, a strangled whimper coming instead of words.

He only nods. "My personal conservatory is open to you when you need it." He reaches around his neck, lifting off a thick band with a light pink crystal at the end shaped to a deadly point. "The Vanegas family is strong, Lana. *My son*, the heir to my empire, is strong." His scarred hands look so large as he holds out the necklace, and my vision blurs as I lean forward, letting him place it around my neck. His warm hand pets my cheek affectionately. "You do not have to be." The weight of the necklace settles on me like a blanket, its dark brown tie so long, it lays at the bottom of my breasts.

My cries fill the conservatory as the blizzard gives way to ice pelting the windows, and he grunts again as he eases himself down onto the couch, resting his head back. "My name is Aurelio. It's nice to properly meet you, *without* having my kneecap dislocated."

The laugh that leaves my lips startles me to the point that I shut it off halfway, letting silence fill the room before I wipe my raw, running nose on my sleeve. "Or being punched in the face."

I can hear the smile in his voice. "Welcome to the family. I'll stay here until my son arrives. It's late; get some sleep."

23
Spring

Whore by In This Moment
Lana, Spring

The rose quartz dangles from my neck as I bend, shifting the dirt around before patting it into place. Even outside, I know the moment my husband fills the space, but I pretend I don't. A smile teases at my lips as his footsteps approach. I know he's doing it for my benefit, that if Christian intended to sneak up on me, I would never know he was there, not until he wanted me to.

He stops inches behind me, but still I ignore his shadow, pretending to be engrossed in the flowers I'm tending. I can already hear the gardeners bitching about me ruining the gardens, but these plants, oddly enough, have healed me almost as much as the man at my back. So Christian and my father-in-law tell them to deal with it while I learn.

A soft grumble comes from behind me as I raise my ass higher than necessary, bending my back more than the situation calls for, hoping he likes the view of my scrap of underwear peeking out from under the light purple skirt I tossed on. Even now, my core aches in the best way, his cum still leaking from me, where he insists it should stay for as long as possible. I have no doubt he can see it glistening on my tacky thighs. I'm still not sure how I feel about my husband's apparent breeding kink, especially now that I know it could result in actual babies. They promptly removed the birth control implant I had when I arrived here months ago, *without* my knowledge. My periods haven't started back up, but that's to be expected. With time, everything will settle.

Liquid heat pools deep in my belly as he bends, his hand tracing a line up my back before gently knotting in my hair, tugging me back up from my exaggerated position. "Careful, wife. The last time I fucked you in the garden, two good men lost their lives."

Blood surges up my neck, spilling a blush on to my cheeks. I open my mouth to respond as the patio doors fling open, Jessie all but hopping out to point accusingly at us. "She should be inside planning your proper wedding, one your family will not be absent from, and *you*, brother, are officially," he pauses to check his watch, "fifteen minutes—"

A slinking shot rings out, Jesse's eyes widening before his head snaps down, blood quickly bleeding through his suit jacket.

Everything next happens all at once. I don't know if it's my scream or the gunshot that alerted the guards, but Christian bellows his brother's name as he rips me from the ground, shoving me towards the patio. "Get to the safe room now!"

I stumble forward before turning back to him. "Come with me!"

"Lana, go!"

My heart stops in my chest as Christian grunts, stumbling forward, a hole punched through his shoulder the second a line of armed men flood out from the wood line. Guards around us drop like flies, and I can't stop screaming. Christian's left arm hangs limp at his side as he grips my neck in a punishing hold.

"Get inside now!" He shoves me again, making me stumble.

Sobs and screams clog my throat as he jerks his gun out of his waistband. Guards from other sections of the compound flood in, but it's not enough. I rip off my cardigan, desperately trying to pack it around Jesse's wound before I bolt inside.

"Aurelio! Aurelio, help them!" I scream as I hit the foyer.

"Lana…"

Tears blur my vision as I stop cold, my chest heaving, that voice injecting ice into my veins. I can't look. I can't fucking move.

"Lana, come now. It's time to go home."

"You fucking bastard! You touch her, and I'll rip your fucking intestines out and use them to string up your fucking mother!" It's my father-in-law's voice that snaps me out of my panic.

Vince's face, if you can call it that, is a gnarly cacophony of scars. Gone is his long black hair and sharp, handsome features, one eye milky white as he holds a gun to the back of Aurelio's head.

"You listen to me, Lana: run!" the proud man bellows. "You run now!" His face is bloodied, his suit ruffled, unfamiliar bodies behind him on the landing.

"Now, Lana, I wouldn't do anything like that. I'm not here for them; I'm here for you. To bring you home."

"I—" My mouth snaps shut as something crashes, and Christian is on top of a man, bludgeoning him with the end of his handgun. Shattered glass scatters around us from where they crashed through the nearby windows.

The moment his eyes meet mine, he lets out a guttural sound filled with so much rage, it nearly liquefies me. "Lana, go!"

The next blow he lands ends in a squelch, the end of the gun denting the man's skull. It's then he sees Vince, and he stills in shock.

"I'm not angry with you, my love. I can't fault you for leaving, not the way you did. I hated my brothers for what they did to you, but it's over now. I won't punish you, you know that, not even for baring your cunt for him!"

I flinch as Vince shoves Aurelio, making him stumble down a few stairs before he rights himself. It's only then that I notice Vince's sorry state, the damage my father-in-law did. Aurelio must be in pain, but it doesn't show. I watch as he readies himself, clenching his fists.

"Speak to her again, and I'll fucking—" Christian bellows.

"Speak to her? She's mine!" Vince screams, his voice going hoarse. "You come to me right now, Lana, or they both die. Look at him. He's bleeding out, he's out of ammo, out of options. You come home, and they live. My purpose is with you!"

The gunfire goes mute all at once as I shake, staring down at my dirty hands, at the soil and blood caked in around the band of my wedding ring.

"Don't you dare, Lana. Don't you do that, princess." Christian begs.

Aurelio jolts forward, jerking a blade from his back pocket, and Vince cries out as it embeds in his thigh. His arm swings in an arc before he levels the gun at Aurelio, spewing a slew of profanity just as his knee gives out, hitting the landing hard.

Christian seethes as his father grunts, working to fight his way up the stairs. "Lana, don't take a step. I'm warning you."

I shudder, begging more guards to show up, for anything to stop this, but the seconds pass like hours, and Vince, in all his madness, finally notices the man at his feet.

"Times up!" he screams, firing a shot into Aurelio before turning the gun on my husband.

I'm shoved to the ground, glass prickling my skin as Christian charges him.

"No! I'll go!" I scream as I grip onto him for dear life, scrambling to my feet, inhaling so deeply, it makes my head light. Soaking in the smell of his aftershave. When he grabs me, locking me into him, I sob, wrenching a hand free the same moment I slam my lips to his, digging my finger into the bullet wound on his shoulder.

Christian bellows, his grip loosening for a second. "Lana, no!"

I scramble over my father-in-law's body towards Vince, vomit surging up my throat the moment his arms surround me. "God, I missed you."

"I don't want to be the breeze," I whisper. His touch is every bit as effective as the acid I burned him with. Aurelio gurgles at my feet. My pulse thudding in my ears.

"Get your fucking hands off her!" Christian roars as he stumbles, blood gushing from the hole in his shoulder.

My hands go steady as I grip the crystal, sinking back into Vince's arms, letting him tug me to him as he buries his nose in my hair, inhaling. Vince always liked the way I smelled. Next, he'll nuzzle my neck, the way he always did. I try not to focus on the visceral hurt on Christian's handsome face as I cant my head back, opening my neck for him. "Call your men off. Please."

Vince groans, his gun still pointed at Christian as he works a device from his back pocket. "Fall out. Now."

My grip tightens on the crystal as I jerk it, the band straining on my neck as it pops. Vince makes an odd, strangled sound as his arm tightens around my throat like a vice, and I twist the crystal in my fingers, stabbing backwards, embedding it in his remaining eye.

He cries out but doesn't drop me like I thought he would. My heart slams into my throat as he brings the gun up awkwardly, trying to point it at me as he sags and stumbles. It goes off once, but I didn't scream. I can't. I fight his hold, barely wiggling free as Christian slams into him, sending us all to the ground. My husband, even in his weakened state, is savage in his assault, and I'm sure Vince is long dead before he rises to his full height, firing five shots into his face... and a few more in his cock.

My breathing is ragged as I try to get to my feet, expecting Christian to pass out any second. Blood is matting his dark, wavy hair, and his green eyes are wild as he turns to face me, stumbling again.

"Christ—" My words are cut off. I was wrong. *I was so wrong.*

He descends on me, caging me to his chest, his hand on my throat in a bruising hold as he presses the hot muzzle of the gun to my temple. "I warned you. I fucking warned you, Lana," he grunts, his voice all venom as he presses it harder, making me whimper. "Why? Why would you do that? Why would you fucking do that to me?"

"I—" I choke.

"I love you. How could you fucking leave me?" His voice is raw and slurred when my hand covers his, pulling the gun away. His mossy green eyes are glossy with emotion as he releases my neck, allowing me to fill my lungs, his handsome face covered in blood as I press my forehead to his. "I need you. Don't you ever, ever fucking do that again! I am nothing, Lana, *nothing* without you."

"I just—"

"Swear to me, Lana."

I press my lips to his, kissing him deeply. "I'm sorry. I swear, never again," I whisper, seconds before he sags in my arms, his weight taking us to the floor again. "Somebody help!" I scream, trying to fight out from underneath him. "Somebody help, please!" I slip in his blood as I roll him to his back, cupping his pale cheeks. "Please, please! Please, don't leave me alone. Somebody, please!"

24

Summer

Lana, Summer

I stare down at Aurelio's crystal hanging around my neck, the light pink standing out against my black dress. The wound in my chest festers, bloodier than ever. Tears stream down my raw, puffy cheeks, the pain not stopping, but I've given myself permission to feel it now. My father-in-law gave me a place to wallow, suffer, and rot, so I've used it. Some days, I need help to remember to brush my teeth. Some days I don't get out of bed; I cry for a long time, and then I don't. Strangest of all, some days, I smile and laugh. I enjoy food, even the kinds I hate.

Riley gives me a short nod with a bright smile from the waiting blacked out car behind me, another SUV pulling in behind ours. I never imagined the timid, weepy young girl who used to cower while she delivered my meals to my prison cell would've ended up my friend. Even past my tears, I try to smile back, knowing she doesn't expect it from me. She's been doing great in her schooling and her recovery is going well, but I secretly wish she would never leave. Judging by the way Jesse watches her from where he's leaning up against the hood of the car, he feels the same.

I've been to more funerals than I can stomach in the last few months, but this one by far hurts the worst. It's a bitter, angry pain I'm trying to breathe through. I fiddle with my wedding ring, needing Christian so badly, it seems to rub salt in all my wounds. You never truly feel the loss of someone, know how essential they were to your soul, until you feel their absence. However brief or long lasting the separation is.

"Princess, I am so sorry." Those words make the breath come easier as his warm, gentle hand grips my chin, angling my head so he can press his forehead to mine. "You shouldn't have been here alone."

I give him a soft smile, kissing him lightly on the lips, and even here, my body hums, wanting more, everything he has to give. "I wasn't alone."

He clenches his jaw. "Still, I'm your husband—"

"Hush, it's fine. You're still getting used to this. You don't have to be perfect, not for me."

Seeing softness bleed into his eyes never fails to give me butterflies, especially knowing it's reserved for me. My head is above water as he tugs me in front of him, wrapping me in his warmth as the breeze shifts my long red hair. It's scorchingly hot today, which seems fitting. It's like everything, no matter how devastating, has come full circle. I can see Mom from the top of the cemetery where we stand, watching the service from afar. Her body is hunched over, still, and she doesn't look my way, not since we first arrived. The look of horror and guilt wasn't the reaction I had expected, but it didn't affect me the way I thought it would. She had to have known who paid for Lewis's remaining medical bills, had some clue about the generous good Samaritan who paid for the lavish funeral, the onyx black headstone reflecting the sun.

I sniffle, letting myself grieve the same person for the hundredth time until I watch Mom stand, a sunflower in her hand that she tosses into the hole they lowered him into. She stands there for so long, I wonder if she'll jump in after him, but she doesn't. She turns and looks up towards me, her arms wrapped tightly around her middle. My heart stops in my chest as she nods, her form blurring. I did everything I set out to do: I saved the sun. I was the best big sister ever, until the end. Even if there were times he hated me, times I resented him just as much, I loved that sweet little boy with the messy hair and bright eyes. I would save him all over again.

"I want to go home now."

"Of course," Christian whispers, pressing a kiss to the top of my head before picking me up.

My head goes light as he cradles me in his arms, looking at me like I'm the most precious thing in the world. My smile is a real one, one I feel in my chest. "You know, you make a pretty good knight after all."

He chuckles, shaking his head. His left arm hurts him most days, but with physical therapy slowly helping him regain full strength, he might have full use again one day. "Anything for you, princess."

The wink he gives me is devastating. All those nights I spent whispering about the faceless knight, the adoring husband who would stand by my side, I never imagined I would have it, that, one day, I'd wake up again.

That one day, I'd look forward to the next.

The end

Afterword

Huge thank you to everyone who read and loved Lana and her bloody knights story! This is to date my darkest book and I broke my own heart a thousand times over writing it. If this wasn't enough for you, no worries there is a bonus chapter coming! Be sure to sign up for my author newsletter so you don't miss it. www.authorcalliemoss.com

As an independent author your rating and reviews mean the absolute world to me. If you have the time, please consider leaving your thoughts in a review!

For details on where to find NSFW art of the church scene check out my author Patreon for access to my full backlog of character and spicy art. http://www.patreon.com/DarkauthorCal

Bathed in Blood Playlist

Limbo – Freddie Dredd

Self-Destruction – I Preval

Freak on a Leash – Korn

Fully Alive – Flyleaf

Coming Undone – Korn

Duality – Slipknot

Closer – Nine Inch Nails

Whore – In this Moment

https://open.spotify.com/playlist/5s7Wj4GnRUpi5MjCpRwaSU?si=3aac334a9197465d&pt=210cb27571d13dcf6e1788c88935075a

Also by

From the author of For the Love of Layla and Pain & Possession comes a new gritty, enemies to lovers standalone full of tension, chases and... organs?

Her- What's worse than needing a life-saving organ transplant as a child? Growing up and realizing your deadbeat dad defaulted on the payments for that organ. He got this heart on loan, and if that sounds like it shouldn't be a thing, you'd be right. It shouldn't be, but here we are. Organ repossessions are on the rise along with the poverty line and I'm desperate to not become another cracked open body in some dark alley. I'm desperate to avoid him... the repo man.

Him- She's fucking gorgeous and painfully easy to find. In any other circumstance, I might have asked her out, fed her, fucked her and then never spoken to her again. Men in my line of work don't stay in the same place for long. Unfortunately for her, I'm the best in the business and I just so happen to be here to repossess her heart. Literally.

For the Love of Layla is a dark psychological stalker romance...

Her - How do you cope when you find out the person you entrusted your heart to is a monster? A wolf in sheep's clothing. I did what I thought was the right, logical thing...I ran. Little did I know nothing was ever going to be that easy and he had no intention of letting me go.

Him - The day she left she took a piece of me, hell she took everything I ever was and ever dreamt of being. I've always been a little...different. Inflicted with a chronic need to fixate on things. Who better to fixate on than the woman who stole my heart the moment she quite literally stumbled into my life. I can't let her go and I will get her back by any means necessary. Even if that means destroying us both in the process. She's mine. Only mine. My little love seems to have forgotten that, it's going to be fun reminding her.

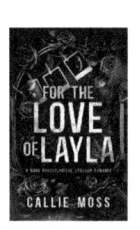